THE HOUSE AT THE EDGE OF THE WORLD

by
Donald Brown

Special Thanks

I would like to thank Shelly Xiao from Jersey School for Girls for her cover illustrations, and Lauren Etchells, another Jersey writer, for her editorial assistance.

CHAPTER ONE

Twelve-year-old Josh Flagsmith stood on the grass below his kitchen window, tossing an old rubber ball against the wall and catching it, as he listened out for the sound of a car. Sandy and his dad should arrive soon to take him out on their boat. Something must have happened to delay them. He brushed back his tousled mop of brown hair and stared down the lane.

He heard the distant drone of a motor approaching from the village. But it didn't sound like his friend's car – more like a van. He waited, ball in hand. The noise had got louder. That van had to be racing down the lane. But why the hurry? Nothing lay beyond the House of the Guardian except a solid wall of mist. So that van must be heading for his house. A sharp niggle of unease pricked at the base of his neck. He shrugged and went on with his game.

Then, voom! He saw a flash of white as the van juddered to a halt outside his front gate. He knew in an instant that something had gone terribly wrong. His arm flew up and the ball hit the window with a crash and a tinkle of glass.

"Hoy!"

In a haze of panic, he saw two colonists in grey jump suits climb out of the van. They had 'CP' printed in big white letters on their chests. The larger one, a clumsy giant, swung open the rear door and more men in jump suits followed. The smaller man walked towards him, notebook in hand.

"Hoy!"

His legs started to wobble. He bent down to pick up the broken splinters of glass, making an effort to control his breathing. "I've broken the window," he mumbled. "Got to clear it up."

"Leave the window and come over here. You're Josh Flagsmith, right?" Six or seven colonists lounged against the side of the van, laughing and making comments. The older one with the swagger and the snide voice seemed to be in charge. He came closer and looked Josh up and down.

"I'm Miggs," he said at last. "You know who we are?"

His mum said 'CP' stood for 'chauvinist pigs' but he guessed that wasn't the answer Miggs wanted so he simply shook his head.

Miggs stared into Josh's face with his sour brown eyes. "We're the new Colonist Police" said Miggs. All right if we have a word with your parents?"

"Yea, sure; except they're not here at the moment." Josh felt sweat breaking out on his face and hands. He thought he remembered Miggs from somewhere.

"So where are they?"

"My parents?"

"I think we were talking about your parents," said Miggs. "What do you think, Osborne?"

"I think we should stop messing around," said the giant with an ill-fitting cap, who took a lazy step towards him. Josh heard more laughter from the men beside the van.

Josh knew he was tall for his age – taller than Miggs – but Osborne towered above him. Faced with his heavy presence, Josh stumbled for an answer. "My parents are out," he stuttered. "My dad always goes to school on Sunday afternoon to prepare his lessons. He's a chemistry teacher you see and…"

"And your mum goes with him? She's into chemistry too, is she? Likes playing around with the old test tubes, does she?" More laughter from the men around the van.

"My mum's at the hospital. She's a doctor and…"

"You're a mouthy little git, aren't you?" said Miggs, jerking him upwards by the neck of his shirt. "What do you think, Osborne? I'd say he's lying. What's that light doing in the upstairs window? That your sitting room?"

"Yes, but my parents are out. I told you!" Josh's voice began to crack.

Osborne went over and leant against the door frame, blocking his retreat. "He's lying," he grunted. "Shall we go inside and drag them out?"

"No, Osborne," said Miggs. "We've got time." He gave Josh a push so that he stumbled and nearly fell. "Don't lie to us, sonny. Tell your parents they've got visitors. We'll wait while they pack their stuff. It won't take them long. They don't need much stuff where they're going."

"What about me?"

The sour eyes examined him. "What do you think, Osborne?" He laughed. "What about the Guardian? Pirates like to give themselves fancy titles, don't they? Don't worry, matey. All in good time." He gave him another push. "In you go then."

Osborne stepped aside to let him through.

Josh edged round him, turning as he entered the doorway. "Where are you taking them?" he asked. His voice had fallen to a whisper.

"To a holiday camp, where else?" said Miggs. Osborne gave a cynical laugh.

Josh stared at him for a second and then slammed the heavy door in his face and raced up the stairs.

His parents sat with their backs to him in the upstairs living room, staring at the telescreen covering the opposite wall.

Reginald Machin, the new chief minister, was speaking. His handsome, hawk-nosed face shone as if it had been laminated.

"Mum, Dad, I need to talk to you."

They glanced at each other. His mum switched off the telescreen and got to her feet.

"What was that noise?" she asked. Her voice sounded too casual. She looked at his stepdad again. They knew! Why hadn't they...?

"It's the new police force. Their van's outside," he blurted out. His stepdad took a few jerky strides to the porthole window overlooking the front entrance. He opened it wide and stared down at the men surrounding the van. "What did they say?" he asked, running a hand through his mat of straw hair.

"They want you to go with them. They said you'd need to get packed."

His parents exchanged glances again. Josh's stomach coiled with suspicion. "What's this about, Dad?"

His stepdad coughed and cast a sideways glance at his mum. "Well, Josh," he said in his schoolteacher's voice, "we knew this might happen but we never expected it to happen so soon. As you know, pirates aren't very popular at the moment; not since Machin's lot won the elections."

Words tumbled out of Josh's mouth like a fizzy drink exploding from a shaken bottle. "Come on, Dad! Half the island are pirates. There are lots of pirate kids at our school. Their parents don't get hassle from the Specials. That's just the have-nots."

"Yes, dear," said his mum quickly. "Let's say the poor and unemployed – most of whom happen to be pirates. She put a hand on his arm. "Look, darling."

He shook it off and turned away. His stepdad stared out of the window. "Machin's declared a state of emergency," he said in a faraway voice.

"And...?"

"He's arresting anyone he sees as a threat to his regime. That includes us, I suppose." He shrugged.

"You know that's not what this is about," his mum said in a quiet voice. "Josh is the Guardian. I warned you they'd do this. They're using us to get to him."

"Yes, yes, dear, I was coming to that!"

Josh felt a hard core of anger forming in his stomach. Those men had come to drag them off to prison. How could they talk like that when their lives were in danger?

"Look, we'll have to do as they say, Josh," said his mum, grabbing his arm. She searched his face for understanding. "It's you we're worried about. We've got to get you off this island before it's too late."

"They're standing by the door," his stepdad cut in, glancing through the porthole window.

Josh stared at him. "I'm going with you," he said. "They can take me to prison too."

His mum's grip on his arm tightened, forcing him to listen. "Please, Josh," she said. "Try to understand! We can't leave this island. It's too late for that. But you can. We've planned for this. Miss Cattermole will be here soon. She's known you since you were so high. She's got an aunt in Crown Colony. She'll take you there tonight. And then to the island of Amaryllis. She'll show you the way."

Josh thought about his young PE teacher, the coolest teacher in his small school. "So the Cat Lady knows?" he asked.

"Yes, Cathy Cattermole knows what we've planned," said his stepdad.

"But Amaryllis is miles away!"

His stepdad turned from the window and Josh felt trapped by the intensity of his gaze.

"Look, Josh," he said. "Pirates on this island are in danger. Amaryllis is the only island that can help us. I meant to go over there and plead with them myself. You'll have to do it for me. Miss Cattermole will explain what you have to do."

A thunderous banging from the floor below jerked them to attention.

"Quickly, Josh," his mum urged, pulling him towards the stairs. He felt the love and tension in her arms as she hurried him towards the front door where those men stood waiting. He wanted to cry for her. "Slip away before they break down that door," she whispered. "Hide round the back of the house till they're gone. And keep a look out in case they come back."

He could hear his stepdad stumbling around upstairs, stuffing a few belongings into a large holdall. Josh lingered with his mum in the dark hallway beside the front door.

"Time's up!" Miggs shouted. "We haven't got all day!"

"We're coming!" she called out in a shrill voice. "We've heard you! No need to break our front door. We're just getting our stuff together. We'll open it when we're ready."

She turned and gave him a last hug. "Listen, have you got everything you need?" she whispered.

"Yes, Mum," he mumbled, wondering what she meant.

"I washed your clothes for you this morning just in case. They're beside your rucksack. Now have you got your stone?"

"Of course, Mum."

"Well, for goodness sake, don't lose it. "Sh! I must go now! Trust us, Josh. We'll see each other again soon! Look! Take this. There's some money inside which you'll need for your journey."

She shoved a small package in his hand and added "Oh, and if those men come back looking for you, run to the end of the garden and hide out in the mist."

"I can't go there, Mum!"

"Nonsense. It might frighten you a little but it's safe. They'd never dare to look for you there. They're too superstitious for that! So will you promise to do that for me – if you need to?"

"Yes, Mum."

"Good. I love you. You know that. This nightmare won't be for long."

His stepdad came down the stairs, dumped his holdall at their feet and clapped Josh on the shoulder. "Run, Josh!" he whispered, pointing towards the back door. "I know you can do this! Hang out there in the garden. Wait for this lot to go and do what your mum says. Hide in the mist if you need to. Miss Cattermole won't be too long."

The banging started again. The thump of a heavy shoulder made the door creak on its hinges. Josh gave his stepdad a hug and ran to the back door, leaving it open a crack, so that he could watch and wait, ready to slip into the mist at a moment's notice.

He heard a voice that sounded like Miggs asking "Where's the boy?" and his mum saying "He's gone. You won't find him," and Miggs, not sounding that bothered, replying "We'll come back for him. We've got time."

Then he heard the shuffle and thump of footsteps and whispered protests from his mum, followed by the roar of the van racing away up the lane.

That was it. They'd gone.

He ran back into the kitchen where he could see the lane leading to the village. Not a car in sight. What was the time? Only three 'o clock in the afternoon. At least if those men planned to return, he'd be able to see them from a distance and have time to plan his escape.

He stared at the broken window. The bare kitchen with its one square table and four chairs seemed empty of life as if Osborne had walked in and swept everything away with a wave of his big fist. He thought of his parents who'd left Amaryllis and settled in this island just to protect him. They didn't deserve to be in prison! The thought brought tears to his eyes.

Mechanically, he stuck his right hand in his pocket. It closed round his stone. He always carried the thing around with him in case he had another epileptic fit. It worked if you held it in your hand when you felt a fit coming on. It would grow warm to the touch and become luminous, so it must have some interior source of power. His mum said it was important, and not just for fits, so perhaps it worked like a computer thing and would guide him on his journey. But in that case why had he never been able to open it?

He laid the stone on the kitchen table and examined it as he'd done so many times before. It was just a small, black onyx ball. There were no buttons you could press and no sign on the polished, round surface to suggest you could open it up and look inside. The more he stared at the object, the more his eyes filled with tears. He had to get off the island. That's what they said. He knew it had something to do with his stone and being Guardian but what did that mean? Was he really supposed to leave his parents in prison and go to Amaryllis? And what then?

He put his hands round the stone and felt it warm to the touch.

"*Josh.*" He started and looked round. It sounded as if someone had called out his name.

"*You're in a bit of a fix.*" He went to the broken window. His heart beat faster, seeing a shadow beside the garage door. A trick of the light; it turned out to be his navy-blue pullover which he'd tossed down at the start of his game. But he still couldn't get that voice out of his head. He looked through the other window, facing onto the lawn and the front gate. The lane led out of sight, empty of life for miles.

"*Josh.*" The sound came from behind him. He started and looked round the room. This didn't make sense. His eyes took in the stove and the fridge and the open kitchen doorway.

"*You asked for advice. Can you hear me?*"

That voice again. It must be coming from somewhere in the room. Then he heard a rattle. The stone on the table had begun to vibrate like a hot coal. He picked it up and examined it more closely. It began to open in his hands and one segment rose and lit up like a computer screen depicting an old man facing him across a desk, staring at him intently over the top of his spectacles. The man looked vaguely familiar, like his sarcastic geography teacher, except he wore a red beret and a black leather jerkin.

"Who are you?" he asked.

"*I'm inside you*," said the dry voice, reaching his ears as if from a distant universe. "*I'm inside the memory of our race.*"

"Can you help me?" he asked, on the verge of tears.

"*How?*"

"I don't know. Can you do magic?"

"I can make traffic lights turn green; except sometimes you have to wait a bit."

"They turn green anyway."

"*There you go then. I can only tell you what's true. This is the stone of truth. Got it?*"

"But I know the truth. My parents have gone to prison and I have no idea when I will ever see them again and I have to get off the island and the Specials could come back any moment."

Another pause. "*That's true.*"

"So can you help me? Please!"

A longer pause this time. Then the same dry voice. "*Well. You asked for advice. This is it. If you want to help save your island and rescue your parents, you've got about a week. Take your choice.*"

"I don't understand. What choice?"

"*You can sit here whingeing or you can go and get ready for your journey.*"

"Thanks a lot!" Josh stuffed the stone in his pocket and stormed off to follow its advice. Did he really hear that bit right about saving the island?

CHAPTER TWO

The Cat Lady should be here soon. Josh ran up to his attic bedroom and stuffed some more clothes into his rucksack. On his way down, he stopped in the sitting room and grabbed a torch from the sideboard cupboard. He stared for a moment through the wide window overlooking the back garden at the grey wall of mist stretching from coast to coast. He watched the plumes of smoky air drifting towards the house and the wispy edges being blown backwards again by the wind. Beyond that lay the central core, solid as iron, stretching from land to sky. He'd only stepped into the mist once and it scared him so much that he had to turn back. But that was when he was a kid. His mum said the fear lay in the mind. The most famous Guardian of them all, Matilda, had placed it there for a purpose. That gave him an edge over the colonists. Their hard-core flat-earthers believed their God created the mist to stop them falling off the edge of the world!

Where was Miss Cattermole? He ran down to the kitchen. From the window above the stove, he had a good view of the village, just a mile away across the moor. Screwing up his eyes, he could see beyond that, to where the island opened out into pastures and more villages. He could see their lights sparkling in the gathering gloom. Beyond that lay 'The Last Resort'; the source of all danger, where white vans now patrolled its silent streets. What if those men jumped back in their van and came for him before Miss Cattermole arrived?

But how would they get to Amaryllis? He remembered the day they left that island by boat, but the journey to Colony Island had lasted weeks. There must be a quicker way. He remembered the drying-up cloth from the sideboard. On one side, the cloth was white except for the blue signature in the bottom right- hand corner, "*Map of the Western Isles, designed by Magnus Maxtrader, Inc.*" He laid it out on the table and turned it over. The islands stretched in a diagonal line from Colony Island in the northwest to the edge of the great continent in the southeast. He followed the diagonal downwards, past some much bigger islands in the centre and found Amaryllis, among a scattering of smaller islands near the bottom of the map. He'd never realised it was that small. And it was miles away. How would he get there in time?

He heard a tap at the front door. That couldn't be the Cat Lady. He'd have heard her car draw up by the front gate. He held his breath as the door creaked open. His eyes darted round the room for a means of escape. Then he heard a high-pitched "Oh!" and a cough and the light tread of a girl entering the hallway.

"Josh," she called out in a clear, posh voice. "I'm looking for Josh."

What if the Cat Lady saw a visitor enter the house? Would she wait or come back later?

That might be too late. He slowly made his way to the door.

A girl stood there in the hallway, looking around as if barging into his house was no big deal. He half-recognised her. She looked a year or two older than himself, with fair skin and long, fair hair, dressed like an adult in a long black skirt and white blouse.

"Well, aren't you going to invite me into your kitchen?" she asked.

"Yea, of course," he mumbled. "Come in."

They sat opposite each other at the plain wooden table. He recognised her now, from the year above him at school. Something didn't feel right about this visit.

"You're Josh," she said, "the young Guardian; the boy whose parents they arrested?"

He nodded. For some reason, she seemed to find him amusing.

"You don't look like a pirate," she said. "Your skin is not much browner than mine."

"I dunno. How are pirates supposed to look? We are not all very dark-skinned, you know. There used to be loads of pirate kids at our school."

"Did there? My stepdad won't let me talk with them, anyway. He says they are all noisy and smelly – not that I think like that." She reached over and placed a pink hand on his, to reassure him. "I'm Lavinia," she added, looking intently at him, still with a slight smile puckering her lips.

"Oh yea, I know you," he said, scenting danger. "You're Machin's daughter."

"Stepdaughter," the girl said with an angry toss of her hair. "It's not the same thing!"

"Sorry, stepdaughter. My dad's a stepdad too." She slowly shook her head.

"Look Josh, I haven't got time for this. It's nice to be sitting here talking to you but I risked my life coming here, so let's get this straight."

As she said it, her eyes flashed as if getting things straight was something she was good at. She placed her left hand with its silver bracelet on the table and used her other hand to grasp each finger in turn to emphasise her points. "Your stepdad's nice. He's a bit spaced out but he's a great teacher and, he means well." She switched hands. "My stepdad is stark raving bonkers. He's hard and mean, and he's never meant well in his life. Do you know what he calls me? 'Slug'." She lowered her voice to a whisper. "And I know for a fact he plans to kill my mum."

Josh jerked to attention. "Really?"

"Really!" she mimicked him. "Not now, he wouldn't because my mum's stinking rich. She's a Maxtrader."

"Oh."

"You knew that, didn't you?"

"No. Sorry."

She shook her head in disbelief. "Don't you know anything? My granddad is Magnus Maxtrader."

"Oh, the one that owns the supermarket chain!"

"And most of the media. Not just here but on Discovery Island and Crown Colony too. The whole Federation. My mum's his daughter. That's why my stepdad married her."

"But I thought you said..."

"He plans to kill her. You'd better believe it! Not now, because he still needs her money, but when he gets his weapon. Then she's finished. You can tell from the way he looks at her."

"Who said anything about a weapon?"

"He did. I heard him talking about it. It's a biological weapon. He reckons that in its concentrated form it will prove lethal. He could use it to wipe out the whole island – or half of it, at least."

"Would he really do that? I mean wipe out half the island?"

She looked cross for a moment. "The pirate half?" she said. "You bet. He's not just playing games, you know. Mind you, his dad was a pirate too. Maybe that's where the hate comes from, but nobody's supposed to know that."

Josh's mind spun in circles. Finally, he asked in a small voice, "How do you know all this stuff?"

"I know everything that goes on in his evil mind." She gave another toss of her fair hair and shuddered. "You have to be tough to stay alive in our house, believe me." Josh believed her. He wouldn't want this girl as an enemy. She gave him a friendly smile, encouraging him to speak.

"Why does he call you Slug?" he asked.

"Because he hates me and he thinks I'm fat and lazy. Why else?"

"But you're not fat!"

"Oh, come on! Don't say you haven't noticed!"

"But you're not! You're..." Josh felt his face reddening. "I mean you're all right." Lavinia smiled. "Thanks. I'll take that as a compliment." She looked down at her skirt. "I look like a teacher in this outfit. Uggh! He makes me wear this stuff, you know."

Josh didn't know what to say. He changed the subject. "How did you get here?" he asked.

"Good question. My stepdad hardly lets me out of his sight except to go to school and church. He's very keen on church, for other people – the Colonist Flat Earth Church. They hate pirates as much as he does, and they're seriously loaded. They helped him win the election because he promised to build a wall round the edge of the world. Some wall! All he's built so far is factories and prison camps. He gets his secretary to drive me to church on Sundays so I persuaded her to drive to your house instead. She's parked further up the road. I had to warn you – you have to get off this island fast. I saw what happened with the CPs, by the way. Have you met their boss?"

Josh shook his head.

"I have. He's called 'Saintly.' He used to be a crime boss called Smith, but he changed it to Saintly-Smith when he became a born-again flat-earther. What a joke!"

"You mean he's not a criminal anymore?"

"Haven't you heard? My stepdad says the best way to abolish crime is to draft all the criminals into the police force."

"What do you mean?"

"Of course he's still a criminal!" She shivered. "It's very cold in here. Do you often go round breaking windows?"

Josh grinned. "Sometimes," he said. Then a sudden doubt struck him. Why were they chatting like this? What if it were a ruse to keep him here until reinforcements arrived? "Won't you get into trouble?" he asked. "If he finds out you're here, I mean?"

"Maria will – that's the secretary. He wouldn't dare touch me yet." She drummed her fingers on the table and glanced at her watch. He noticed she didn't seem too worried about Maria.

"When are you leaving?" she asked.

"You know about that?"

"They'll be coming back to look for you soon. We haven't got long. What are you planning to do?"

Josh studied her face in confusion. He decided to risk it. "I dunno. I have to get off the island somehow. And then Miss Cattermole's taking me to Amaryllis."

She nodded and glanced at the drying-up cloth. "I see you've been planning your journey." She pointed at a dot in the bottom right- hand corner. "That's Amaryllis, where all pirates came from originally, isn't it?" she asked. "That's where you were born. What's it like?"

"I don't remember much. I was six when my parents brought me here."

"Is it true they call you the special one?"

Josh felt his cheeks going hot. He shifted in his seat, taking a quick peek out of the window for that little red sports car. "I dunno," he said. "Not round here, they don't. Special in what way?"

Lavinia leaned towards him. "Come on! You must know! Everyone else does. You have the gift. You've got telepathic powers. Isn't that what they call them?" Josh thought of the pain and desperation he felt before using his stone to control one of his epileptic fits. He'd only just learned that his stone could be made to open and reveal things.

"I don't know. I've only tried them once," he said.

"Well, you should. They could be a lot of fun; especially if you tried them on my stepdad." She shook her head and smiled. "Poor boy! You don't know much, do you?" she said. She reached into the pocket of her skirt and handed him an envelope, watching his reaction as he took it from her. She leant forward and grasped his hand. "Listen, Josh," she said. "We're in this together. We've got to help one another. That's why I'm here. My mum's in danger and your parents too. We've got to stop him."

"How?"

Josh glanced out of the window again. What if this girl had been sent to spy on him? He'd told her too much already, but he wanted to trust her.

She squeezed his hand. "Are you listening, Josh? Will you stop in Crown Colony?"

"I think so."

"You must stop there if you're heading for Amaryllis. Well, when you stop there, you must speak to my granddad – you know, Magnus Maxtrader. Give him this letter. At least that's a start."

"Will he listen?"

She laughed. "Probably not," she said. "He's about as warm and cuddly as a hard-boiled egg. You'll just have to convince him that my stepdad's bad for business, which he is." She stood up.

"How will I find him?"

"He's always on his yacht. Just barge in and ask to see him. That's what I'd do!"

"What about my parents?"

"I don't know. They're safe for the moment because my stepdad still needs them to get to you. I'll think of something. I'll let them escape...somehow."

"But where, when, how?"

She didn't seem too sure about that. She looked around, in a hurry to leave. She seized his hand. "I don't know, Josh. I'll do my best, right?"

Josh smiled. This girl certainly had a nerve! But then again, Maxtrader was her grandfather. He stood up and followed her to the door.

"Is that it? How will we stay in touch?" She grabbed his arm. "Don't try to contact me whatever you do. He has spies everywhere. Unless maybe through your stone?"

"So you know about that too?"

She shook her head. "You really don't get it, do you? My stepdad talks about you all the time; 'the young Guardian'. He likes to think he's really modern but he's superstitious like crazy. He thinks, once he's got rid of you, pirates will give up their resistance."

"So why didn't he arrest me with my parents?"

She gave him a curious look. "I'm not sure you really want to know," she said.

"Yes, honestly."

"Honestly," she mimicked him. "Poor boy! Let's say he didn't want you in prison. He wanted you out of the way." She gave a frown of impatience and added, "Out of the way, as in dead. Get it?" She glanced at her watch again. "Look, I really must fly! High fives? We depend on each other, right?"

She held up her hand for Josh to tap and then changed her mind, gave him a quick hug and hurried out of the house.

CHAPTER THREE

J osh sat at the table, lost in the pleasant warmth of that hug. Then his stomach lurched at the memory of that word, 'disappear'. He ran to the window. No sign of anyone. It would be dark soon. What if they were watching the house and Miss Cattermole couldn't get through?

A thump at the front door jolted him to his feet. That couldn't be her. He'd have heard her car. He dashed upstairs to the landing, where a small window opened over the porch. He stood poised for his next move; to slip out the back way and hide in the mist. His legs quivered with alertness. Whoever had knocked at the door didn't intend to knock twice. Had he found a way of entering the house unseen?

Then he saw it; the faint shadow of a human presence obscured by the porch roof. He jumped away from the window, nearly stumbling over a chair.

"Is that Josh?" called the shadow.

"Sandy!" he cried, "Hold on! I'll open the door."

But why Sandy? Did he still think they were going off in his dad's car?

Sandy lumbered into the kitchen, shaking rainwater from his back like a Labrador fresh from a swim.

"What are you doing here, Sandy?"

Sandy's honest, freckled face looked round the room in a puzzled sort of way. "I dunno," he admitted. "Bertie sent me. I heard him talking with my dad. They changed their mind about the Cat Lady for some reason and sent me instead."

Josh didn't know anyone called Bertie. The name didn't inspire him with confidence. What happened to the Cat Lady? Now he had to get to Amaryllis with the help of Sandy and a man called Bertie.

But they had to go now! Those men could return any moment!

He stared through the window as Sandy parked his solid frame at the kitchen table and spread the jumbled contents of his rucksack over the plain, pine surface. "I've brought some provisions," he said.

"Great."

Josh nodded distractedly.

Sandy opened his plastic container, peered inside and then hesitated. "Except I've eaten them," he said.

"Oh."

"I've got a banana."

Josh sighed and stared out of the window again. His friend was always like that. It was no use trying to hurry him. "Thanks. Sandy," he said, "how did you get so wet?"

Sandy waved an arm in the direction of the back garden. "I came that way."

"What? You came through the mist?"

Sandy paused and thought about it. "It was a bit misty, I suppose."

"You mean you didn't feel anything – like some force or other holding you back?"

"What sort of force?"

"I don't know. It sort of saps your energy. When I tried it, I could hardly move."

"It was quite wet," said Sandy lamely. "They said it wouldn't harm me as I don't have that thing that most people have got, which makes them afraid of things."

"Imagination?" suggested Josh.

"I think they used a word like that," agreed Sandy. "I only skirted the mist," he added. "I used that new compass your father lent me. My dad said it would be safer to take this route because these flat-earth types wouldn't follow me there. Bertie's house is just over there," he said. He pointed to the right of the lane where you could just see a white house at the top of the cliffs. "But we can't go that way," he said, "or else they'd find us."

Josh nodded. He kept an eye on the kitchen window. Those men could come back any moment. "These flat-earth types," Sandy continued. "What I don't understand about them is they think we live at the edge of the world, right? But then why is Machin sending barges round the headland? I mean, I thought those barges were meant to be patrolling the edge of the world, to stop ships from falling off."

"I don't know," Josh said, only half listening. "Does the mist extend over the sea?"

"My dad says that it does for a bit but it's still possible to get round it. And that's what he thinks Machin's doing. My dad says that he's got loads of men working there, in the land beyond the mist; mostly pirates, my dad says. Slave labour, he calls it."

"Really? Maybe the flat-earthers don't realise what he's up to."

Sandy nodded. "My dad says...."

Josh sighed and stood up. He lifted his rucksack onto the table, ready to move off. He went over, one last time, to the broken window and stared up the lane leading to the village. "I think we're safe for the moment," he said.

Sandy didn't seem to hear him. "What would happen to the ships?" He continued. "I mean, you would think that before they even got near the edge, they would feel an enormous force tugging them downwards. My dad says they must be a little bit mad. I wonder what Reginald Machin sees in them."

"Loads of money, probably. Anyway, what have you got in your rucksack?"

"I've got this rope. I thought it might come in useful in case… well, in case we needed it. And this knife. And a ball of twine and my binoculars…"

"What's this pistol doing? Do you know how to fire it?"

"It's my dad's starting pistol. He didn't want me to take it. But I told him we might need it in case we got attacked by a man or a dog, for example. It's not really dangerous unless you are standing right in front of it but it makes quite a noise. Would you like me to show you?"

"No thanks, Sandy, put it down. Please!"

Sandy sat down again and placed the pistol on the table, looking a bit crestfallen.

Josh heaved his rucksack onto his back. "Well, I've got my stuff packed so let's go," he said. "Do you know how to get to that place?"

"The Hilltop Farm?" asked Sandy. He still hadn't moved from the table. "That's what Bertie's house is called. We just have to double back through the mist and then follow the line of the cliffs. Bertie's a friend of my dad. He's expecting us. He'll get you off the island, I suppose."

"Good. Let's go out the back way in case anyone spots us from the road."

He led Sandy along the dark hallway leading to the rear of the house where another door led into the back garden. He pointed towards a rickety white gate at the end of the garden where a thin trail snaked through the undergrowth towards the wall of mist. He'd never thought of it as a place of safety before.

Sandy pushed his way ahead. "Yes, that's the way I came just now."

Josh smiled. If Sandy could do it, so could he! He followed his friend into the first grey swirling wisps of mist. If the

Guardian made that mist four hundred years ago, maybe another Guardian could pass through it unharmed.

He kept one hand in his pocket, tightly gripping the stone, as he felt the mist closing around him. Ghostly shadows dipped towards him, blocking his path, and vanishing. He thought he heard mocking laughter, but it could have been the wind whining through the trees. The stone felt warm in his hand and the sight of Sandy plodding on ahead gave him strength.

He followed in Sandy's footsteps, puffing and panting through bracken and reedy swamps, barely able to see the path beneath his feet. Sandy barged ahead, splashing through the swamps and waiting every fifty yards or so, when he came to a dry stretch of bracken. The further they moved into the mist, the tighter Josh clutched his stone, struggling to fight off the clammy fingers of despair that clung like ivy to his chest.

"There's a clearing just ahead," Sandy said. "I remember it from earlier. We can stop there and get our breath back." He pointed to a tall silver birch tree with a circle of dry mud and twigs around its trunk. As soon as he stopped going forwards, Josh noticed that the mist released its grip. He could breathe more freely, resting his back against the trunk of the tree while Sandy sat on a fallen log and fiddled with his compass.

"That thing doesn't look like a compass," said Josh. "It's just a stone in a sort of silver disc." He noticed a flashing arrow on the rim. "How does it know where to point?" he asked.

Sandy shrugged. "I dunno," he said. "It seems to follow my thoughts."

The arrow suddenly turned a full circle and pointed in the direction they'd just come.

At that moment, Josh heard the distant drone of two helicopters approaching from the east. "What's all that about?" he asked. "There's nothing here."

"Except us," agreed Sandy.

"Yes, I know, but what are they looking for?"

Sandy looked up. "I think it's time to move."

"But you haven't answered my question!"

"Oh, that! I think they are looking for us. Or you, really."

"You must be joking!"

Sandy looked anxious. Josh remembered that Sandy didn't do jokes. He looked back at the house. He felt the sound of the helicopters pressing in on him. And beyond that soldiers on foot perhaps, like beaters. It was like that girl had said. In their eyes, he was the special one! He thought of his parents. What if the police used his parents to get to him? They could be sitting in a cell at that moment while Osborne beat the truth out of them. He pushed the thought away but the image kept coming back.

Sandy was still talking. "My dad said they planned to pick you up. You're the Guardian. That's why I had to come here early."

"But why helicopters? Why not just send a van to collect me?"

"Maybe they sent a van and you weren't there. Maybe we left just in time. Anyway, they're not trying to collect you. They're trying to..."

Josh wanted to change the subject fast. "What will they do now?" he asked.

"I dunno. I suppose they'll land soon and start searching the house."

Josh looked back and imagined armed thugs trampling through every room. Then he thought of his own, small attic bedroom crammed with all his favourite junk. Would he see his house again and, if he did, would it ever feel the same?

"What if they come after us now?" he asked.

"I don't think they will. Not in this direction. It's the mist, you see. It doesn't seem to affect me. But I know most people are afraid of it."

"Well, I'm afraid of it."

"Yes, but you've got that stone thing."

"How did you know that?"

"My dad told me you'd be carrying it. It's called the stone of truth. It's supposed to protect you against mist and things."

Josh felt in his pocket where the small stone warmed to the touch. Despite the fright it had given him, the stone gave him a curious sense of strength and comfort. He knew that he'd never have been able to get this far through the mist without it.

"Where next?" he asked, standing up.

"This is the hard part. We have to double back towards the cliffs, away from this mist. It's open ground too, where the enemy could spot us. Follow me. I remember this bit from before."

Josh hurried after Sandy along a narrow path that wound its way through gorse and bracken and brambles towards the salty air of the sea. It felt good to get away from the mist. Soon he could smell the sea breeze and see the line where the trees and yellow gorse bushes ended in a ploughed field leading down to the cliffs.

Sandy stopped and pointed in the direction of the sea. "This bit's open to the sky but there's no helicopters around at the moment. We'll have to do it at a run. I'll show you."

Sandy plunged through the sodden clay like a frog through an oil slick, with his heavy boots sticking out sideways and clogging in the soil. Josh felt a release of energy, now that the mist lay behind them. He gave his friend a head start, and then swept past him with light-footed ease, turning back to applaud Sandy's progress with a slow handclap from the shade of a holm oak on the other side of the field.

"Where next?"

Sandy pointed to a field of gorse and bracken leading down to the cliff's edge. Without Sandy there to guide him, Josh might have missed the path entirely and stepped from grass into misty air. A little way to his left, Sandy pointed to some steps leading downwards to a narrow ledge two metres below the top of the cliff. Josh followed him down the steps and found himself staring at a sheer drop down bare chalky cliffs to an angry, foaming sea. He grabbed Sandy's arm. "Let's keep moving. Is this the path?"

"Yea. It's a bit dodgy in places so you have to take it slowly."

Sandy led the way. The path looked safe enough if you leant into the cliff and checked carefully where you placed your feet, treading on tufts of grass to avoid the slippery stones. There was just enough space to plant both feet side by side on the path and there were even occasional resting places carved out of the rock where there was space for two people to admire the downward view, if they were suicidally inclined.

He kept his eyes on Sandy's back and the cliff face to his left, holding up a hand to grasp any plant or projecting rock which would steady him and take the weight off his feet. As long as he didn't let his eyes stray to the right, he found the path easy enough. They walked on in silence for several minutes.

Then Sandy stopped. "Now comes the difficult part," he said. "Oh! Damn!"

"What's the matter, Sandy?"

"Someone's been here before us. They've taken the bridge away."

The path widened at this point. Josh walked forward and put an arm on Sandy's shoulder. Then he saw what Sandy was looking at. The path in front of them had gone.

He peered into six feet of swirling mist and wind and, beyond that, a jagged rock where the path started again on the other side.

They couldn't go on. But what if they went back? Choices! They didn't have a choice!

Josh walked past Sandy, right up to the edge, and looked down the cliff, down and down, past the circling seagulls, to the distant waves battering against the rocks in an angry white froth. He quickly stepped back, pulling Sandy with him. His friend's face had gone white.

"There were planks there before," said Sandy. "Look. You can see what's happened."

Josh looked across the gap at the three planks tossed in the grass beyond their reach. Somebody had done that in the last few hours.

"I don't really mind heights." Sandy mumbled. He sat with his back to the gap – a clear sign that he wasn't going anywhere. "It's depths I'm afraid of."

"So am I." Josh knew in his heart that turning back wasn't an option. He had to be brave like his parents. He owed it to them to get to Crown Colony. He'd jumped more than six feet before; ten feet was his best effort. "I suppose with a rope," he said at last. "Have you got a rope?"

"What do you want to do?" Sandy mumbled. He still had his back to him.

"If you tied one end round your waist – like in mountaineering – then I've got the other end and if I fall, you can hold my weight. I did that once with my stepdad."

"What happened?"

"I fell. I bashed my arm on the rocks, but it was quite safe really. If I can make the jump, I can replace the planks from the other side and you can walk across like you did last time."

"Are you sure you can do this?" asked Sandy.

"Yes. I'm the one that can jump. Remember?"

He measured up his run, taking a few trial steps as he would for the long jump at school. It was no good. Mesmerised by the act of looking down, he started to shake.

"Are you ready?" Sandy had turned to face the gap, leaning back with his strong hands grasping the rope.

"Yes," said Josh in a sudden trance. "It's our only choice."

He eyed the spot some three feet clear of the gap on the other side where he intended to land, counted aloud to three, ran forward at gathering speed and launched himself into the air.

Help! The moment his feet left the ground, it came to him in a flash. He had fallen short; barely managing to grasp the rock on the other side. His feet were flailing in no man's land, dragging his weight backwards down the abyss. He guessed in that moment that even Sandy might not have the strength to halt his sudden plunge. His hands scrabbled for a better hold. He threw all the strength of desperation into his arms and shoulders and urged his whole body forward until his centre of balance shifted and he was able to scrabble over the rock onto the grass beyond. He lay there for a while panting and shaking.

Replacing the planks wasn't as easy as they'd imagined. In the end, by lying flat on either side of the gap, they managed to haul each plank into place with the aid of the rope. Sandy eventually crawled across, with the rope secured round his waist and Josh holding the other end.

They paused while Sandy detached the rope, then set out on the last leg of their journey. Now that his scare was over, Josh felt flushed and confident, struggling up the slope with Sandy plodding along behind.

"Josh! Sandy! We're over here!" The sound of a man's voice awoke him from his thoughts. It came from some distance away at the top of the cliffs.

"That's Bertie," said Sandy.

Looking up, Josh saw a lantern flickering and what looked like two figures, one much smaller than the other. They stood on an open grassy headland where the cliff path ended, and the cliff turned back on itself and ran sharply downwards towards a rocky bay.

"You took a long time in coming." It was the girl who spoke first. Her dark eyes flashed with attitude. She looked a bit like a gipsy child with her unwashed face and untidy black hair. She wore just a striped tee-shirt and jeans with a beret perched jauntily on her head. She could have been a year or two younger than him; but she looked like trouble.

"Come on, Megs, be nice to the kid. He's going to be our guest. Shake hands now like a lady."

"He's not having my room," Josh heard her mutter.

"Don't worry, I'm not staying," was the best he could manage but it seemed to cheer her up a bit.

Bertie clapped Sandy on the shoulder. "Your dad's here, old chap," he announced. "He's taking you home before it gets dark." Bertie wore a beret like Megs and a navy-blue pullover which rounded over his stomach. He rubbed his hands together, murmuring "Well, this is nice" – as if Josh were a long- awaited guest and not a boy wanted by the police and fleeing for his life.

Chapter Four

J osh saw a whitewashed bungalow with a few ramshackle
outbuildings set in the brow of the hill and, beyond that, a
narrow causeway leading to the old fort, which got surrounded
by the sea at high tide.

He followed Bertie through a low arched doorway down some
stone steps into a long dark room. The walls were of bare stone
with a few sticks of furniture scattered over a threadbare carpet.
Left of the entrance he saw two high-backed armchairs with
fading flower patterns either side of a large empty fireplace.

Once inside, Bertie became a different person. His broad face
creased with worry. His eyes darted round the room and he
muttered, "We've got so little time." He grabbed his computer
from the sideboard and shouted, "Megs! Have you packed your
stuff? Good! You can go with Sandy as far as the brow of the hill
where the bus stop used to be. His dad's waiting for him there.
You know where I mean, don't you? But get back as quick as
you can!"

Megs grinned and led Sandy out of the house, talking to him
all the time in giggles and whispers.

The room went silent with Megs' departure. Josh looked
around, waiting for some sort of a signal from Bertie. "This
place has gone downhill a bit since my old mum left," Bertie

said. His smile formed friendly creases at the corner of his eyes. "Have a seat anyway – over here by the fireplace."

Josh sat upright in his high-backed chair and let his eyes wander round the room, feeling friendless after Sandy's departure. Bertie strode over and sat in the armchair opposite, bringing his computer with him. He wanted to know all about the arrest of Josh's parents and his journey through the mist, but he seemed tense and fidgety. Josh sensed that he was only half-listening. He kept looking at his watch and checking his computer screen. Finally, he stood up and went to the window. "They're onto us," he said, with a sigh. "I wish that girl would do what she's told. She should be back by now."

"Do they know where we are?" asked Josh

"No, but they know where we're heading," said Bertie.

"So what are they doing now?"

"They've lost the trail for the moment. They can't work out how you escaped without being seen. They're still combing the area. They will stop that soon and head out here."

"Why are we going to the fort?" asked Josh.

"That's where my boat's moored," explained Bertie. "Besides, it's the only way off the island because of the roadblocks. You're an important fellow, you see!"

"Is that why Megs…?"

Bertie laughed. "You mustn't mind Megs," he said. "She is a bit of a rebel and she thinks we're giving you too much attention."

He came and sat down again. "But she's a good kid if you dig deeper," he said. "Anyway, where on earth has she got to? We have to leave in a moment."

"Am I meeting Miss Cattermole?"

"Not sure about that," said Bertie. "No doubt we'll hear from her soon."

What was Bertie not telling him? Josh felt sure she'd be involved in his escape. Otherwise, he'd have to rely on Bertie, who seemed nice enough but a bit unsure about things, and Megs, who'd taken an instant dislike to him. Was this really the plan that his parents had arranged for him?

He noticed Bertie observing him in a friendly way, waiting for him to speak. "Is Megs your daughter?" he asked him.

Bertie laughed. "No, bless her," he said. "She's an orphan. Her parents were friends of ours so my mum took her in when they died."

"Is your mum…?"

"She's not here any longer. They took her away." His voice sounded flat. He stared into the middle distance, as if remembering how things used to be.

"Why?"

Bertie shrugged. "Everything's changed since Machin won the elections. It's all happened very quickly. Pirates don't have a voice anymore. Those men didn't give a reason. They don't have to. They just came and picked her up like a piece of old furniture and drove her off. Poor old mum! She used to run this place, you know.

Josh still couldn't get his head round it. "Why does it matter?" he asked. "Whether you're a pirate or a colonist?"

"Don't ask me! Unemployment, I suppose. Somebody's got to shoulder the blame. We have shared the island for the past three hundred and seventy years. That's when the first colonists arrived, isn't it?

Josh hardly heard him. The words seemed to be coming from far away. He was thinking of that smashed window, Bertie's mother being hauled off to prison and then Osborne and the man with the snide voice and his parents being driven off in a white van.

"Something the matter, old chap?" asked Bertie.

"What? Oh, I see what you mean. I was wondering what my parents were doing now and when I'd get to see them again and if they're – you know – coping with being in prison and–"

Bertie's tone was reassuring. "Let's see," he said. "How long have they been gone? Two hours? They're safe at the moment. I'm sure of that. Machin knows he can't touch them yet. Besides, he needs them as a bargaining counter." He glanced quickly at Josh and looked away again. Josh fingered the stone in his pocket. He knew what Bertie meant. Machin's lot were after him because he was Guardian and that was because of his stone. He hadn't thought much about his stone – not since he was six years old and had his first fit – but he needed to think about it now. The dizziness and fear of that first fit came back to him in a sudden wave of nausea. He pictured the crowded room in Amaryllis and his parents' friends towering over him, and a woman who shrieked, "It's true! The boy has the gift! Our new Guardian has come at last!" People said afterwards that they hadn't seen a case of temporal lobe epilepsy for a hundred years. That was his gift!

Being Guardian must mean more than that. All he remembered was waking up in a hospital ward strapped to a bed, with a cloth between his teeth to stop him biting his tongue, and his mum rushing into the ward and thrusting the stone into the palm of his hand, and the immediate relief he felt, as if the stone had the power to suck all the dizziness out of him. Then he'd suddenly become famous. That's why his parents had brought him to this island so that he could grow up in peace. His mum had trained as a doctor after that, specialising in paediatrics. She told him that meant children's illnesses.

But the stone meant more than that. It must do. He'd seen the way it opened up for him like some miniaturised computer and he winced as he thought of that dry old voice telling him to stop whingeing.

Then he looked up and noticed that Bertie had gone outside. He returned in an instant, shaking his head about something. "No sign of that girl yet," he said. "Still, I have another way of getting you off this Island, if needs be." The thought seemed to settle him and he returned to his armchair. "Is something worrying you?" he asked Josh. .

"I was thinking about my stone."

"That's a precious object you've got there," said Bertie. "They say it's more than four hundred years old. They were advanced in those days."

"Is it like a computer?"

"Better than that, I'm told," said Bertie. "It only works for you, mind. That's because you share Matilda's genes. You know about genes, right?"

"My dad explained it to me once; he's a chemistry teacher, but I'm not really into chemistry," Josh admitted. "I know we were both epileptic."

"Have you tried to open it?" asked Bertie. "Only the Guardian can do that."

"It opened for me once," said Josh, thinking of that sarcastic old man who told him not to whinge. "But it happened just like that. I don't know if I could do it normally."

They both leapt to their feet as a bedraggled Megs burst into the house.

"Megs!" cried Bertie. "Where on earth have you been?"

"It's the truancy officers," Megs explained, halfway between panting and sobbing. They are on the way to the house. They've got the 'pigs' with them."

For a moment Josh almost felt sorry for her.

"How many are they?" asked Bertie.

"Just two of them. A man and a woman. And a few officers. The woman called me a 'wretched aborigine!' Well, that was after I bit her arm," Megs added, with a defiant stare.

Bertie stood over her and sighed, like a weary parent going through the motions of telling off an impossible child. "I warned you about this. You were supposed to go to school this morning, like any normal kid. Now you've alerted the whole neighbourhood. Listen, they'll be here any minute! Come on! Megs! Josh! Follow me!"

"How long have we got?" asked Josh. "I mean before the causeway gets flooded?"

Bertie looked at his watch. "It's too late to worry about that. The enemy will be out there watching it now. We'll have to take another route."

"Plan B?" asked Josh. His stepdad was a fan of Plan B.

Bertie stopped and pointed. "You could call it that. See that door on your right which leads into the kitchen? As you go through, you'll see a blank wall with an oil painting of my old mum, when she was just a girl. Behind that is the entrance to a secret passage."

Josh liked the idea of a secret passage, but not when it was Plan B.

"I wouldn't recommend it if we had a choice," said Bertie. This used to be a smugglers' house. They used it to store the goods they dropped off at the old fort. They already had a disued well so they bore a hole at the bottom of the well and constructed an underwater passageway leading to the fort. The passageway is solid enough but to reach it we have to descend an iron ladder fixed to the wall of the well. Some of the steps have rusted away over time. Come on, Megs. You too, Josh, of course. Quickly! They'll be through that door any moment."

Bertie hurried them though the picture frame into the dark, draughty space beyond the door. The three of them squeezed round the narrow ledge surrounding the well. It was just possible to sit with their feet up, and their backs against the wall, without touching the rim; four shadows hunched up in the semi-darkness.

Josh leant forward and peered into the well. Row on row of red bricks, stained with green algae, spiralled downwards into the darkness.

"Choices," thought Josh. No need to ask the stone's advice on this one. "Has anyone tried this recently?" he whispered, peering down into the void. His question echoed alarmingly from the depths of the well.

"Chicken?" suggested Megs.

"Chicken! Chicken!" sounded the echo.

Josh glared. He could see from her smile that she'd got the reaction she wanted and he felt a sudden urge to push her over the edge.

"I tried it once," she said.

"You did?" Bertie looked shocked. "We warned you about the dangers!"

"Well, I only tried a few steps. Some of the rungs are a bit dodgy but the sides of the ladder are solid. So there!" she added, her dark eyes flashing with mischief.

Bang! Crash! Tinkle!

The sound came from the front door. They all froze.

The police, thought Josh. They liked smashing things. He heard the angry shouts of a crowd breaking into the room where they'd been sitting moments before. He looked at the tense faces surrounding the well and made up his mind. He edged his way round the ladder projecting from the rim, grasped the sides firmly and put his feet on the first step.

"Are you sure you can manage?" whispered Bertie.

"I'm ok." He put his weight on the step.

"Be careful!"

"I'm fine!"

Crack!

Silence.

A thump as the broken step reached the bottom of the well.

"What happened? Are you all right?"

Josh's heart thumped wildly. His legs kicked helplessly into space but he still had a firm grip on the sides of the ladder while his feet scrabbled for a hold on the step below.

"Are you all right?

He listened to the hollow echo and said "Yea, it gets safer after the first steps."

Seized by an idea, he eased the heavy rucksack off his shoulder, gripping one side of the ladder with one hand and reaching out with the other to hold the rucksack by its two straps. Gently, he lowered it until the weight nearly forced him to topple over and lose his grip on the ladder. He steadied himself and brought the rucksack round in front of him where he was able to retrieve his torch. That was all he needed. Not trusting himself to get the rucksack back on his shoulders, he simply let it fall.

He didn't hear it hit the bottom.

And then, a few moments later, he heard a thump.

"What was that?" The echo from above.

"Nothing. Just my rucksack. Watch this!"

Moments later, the torch started to flicker and fill the sides of the well with light. He could see Bertie's round, anxious face peering over the edge of the well and, when he looked down, he could see the dank circular brick walls stretching downwards seemingly forever.

"Bertie, can you hear me?" he called.

His voice was greeted by an echoing reply. "I hear you! I thought for a moment that you'd fallen!"

"No way! The ladder's safe – I'll wait for you at the bottom!"

After the echoes of his speech died away, he heard whispering above and Bertie, with his computer securely strapped around his waist, began his awkward descent. Josh gripped the sides of the ladder, imagining what might happen if Bertie slipped and tumbled down on top of him. He saw Megs quickly scramble after Bertie. The light was enough to illuminate their shadows above him descending the circular brick walls.

Still, the sides of the ladder held firm. This gave him confidence. In fact, he became so absorbed in the act of descent that, when he reached the bottom, it felt as if the concrete floor rose up and hit him. He picked up the rucksack he'd dropped and waited.

Soon the others joined him, and Bertie led the way down the dark, flag-stoned passage that ran beneath the causeway and ended up within the walls of the old fort. At one point, Meg grabbed Josh's hand and, looking up into his face, asked, "Are you still mad with me?"

The question took him by surprise. "No, why?" he asked.

"Well, you should be," she said. "You're not as bad as I thought."

He squeezed her hand, thinking, "and neither are you." He wondered how he would feel if his parents were dead, and not just in prison, and he had to fend for himself in a dangerous world.

CHAPTER FIVE

L avinia stepped out of her chauffeured car outside the gates of the New Academy. She screwed up her face and smoothed it down with her hands like a plastic mask. She loved that half hour in the car, chatting with Maria. It ranked with the hour or so at the end of the day in the privacy of her bedroom. Best of all was when her mum knocked on her bedroom door and they shared a few moments together talking about the good times they'd had together, just the two of them, before the BIG MISTAKE.

She kept her head down to avoid attention from her red-jacketed classmates hurrying into the assembly hall. She followed them through the glass-fronted entrance lobby lined with portraits of the New Regime. In the centre, a large oil painting of her stepdad beamed down on her. Underneath the portrait was the New Party election manifesto that she knew by heart:

"A new approach to crime

A new approach to education

A new approach to jobs

March ahead with Machin!"

Yea. Sweeping innocent pirates off the streets and sticking them in prison; that was a new approach!

She hurried after the crowd of chatting, jostling school kids, down the long corridor smelling of fresh paint and disinfectant through the wide swing doors and into the back of the assembly hall. She slipped into a space at the end of the dimly lit back row and peered through the semi-darkness at the rows in front of her. She couldn't see the tall boy with the tousled mat of brown hair and the twinkling eyes. She clenched her fists. Good. He must have got away. Her hands tightened. But what if it meant they'd caught him?

She looked at the stage. The new headmistress appointed by her stepdad, Miss Brassmould, sat in the centre with her staff lined up behind her. Half of the staff were new too. They were the ones who wore 'New Party' stickers on their shirts and clapped the loudest when the reverend Billy Swagger of the Flat Earth Church strode to the rostrum. Billy Swagger was a short, chunky colonist preacher with a shiny pink face and shiny black hair whose church had helped fund her stepdad's election campaign.

"The lesson this morning," he roared, "is taken from *The Book of Colonists,* chapter one, verse one:

'And on the third day, God looked at the land he'd created which was all round and full of crinkly bits and said, they will never be able to walk on that! So he smoothed it out with his almighty hands and set a mist round the edge of the world so that they wouldn't fall off.'"

Some of the older kids in the back rows started to laugh; probably pirates, thought Lavinia. They'd be in trouble for that. Her attention wandered to the long line of teachers at the back of the stage. Behind Miss Brassmould, she spotted Catherine Cattermole. But Miss Cattermole shouldn't be there! She should be in Crown Colony by now with Josh Flagsmith! Did that mean they'd caught him? But then they'd have caught the Cat Lady too! There must be some other explanation. There must!

Billy Swagger shut his heavy book with a thump and leaned over the lectern. "You know, I'm a simple man," he said, "but to me it's all there in *The Book of Colonists*." He gazed into the middle distance and smiled in wonder at the simplicity of his faith. Then he returned to his audience and said, in a reasonable voice, "Now I know there are some people who say the earth is round. You know the sort of people I mean? Liberals, intellectuals, people with limp handshakes. Well, to these people I say, if the earth's round, how come the sea doesn't fall out of its basin and wash all over us? How come we don't spend all the time walking uphill, or downhill for that matter? No, our bible tells us like it is. Let's take a moment to thank the Lord for the flat earth he has given us and for that wonderful mist that stops us from falling over the edge."

He bowed his head in silent prayer. Then, raising his head, he announced: "I want to end my address with a short hymn, which I think you all know. I'm going to say the words once, and then we will try and sing it together:

'When God made our feet, he placed them on the ground.

He didn't make them curved and he didn't make them round.

We all know the reason why he didn't do that.

He wanted us to walk on a world that's flat.'

All together now!"

Lavinia closed her mouth and scowled as four hundred kids bawled out the words, aided by the young music mistress, Cecilia Prune, whose pigtails bobbed up and down as she thumped on her piano. Then the preacher took a bow and let the headmistress take his place at the lectern.

Miss Brassmould cleared her throat. Her booming voice and huge bust provoked the usual sniggers. She pursed her lips, waiting for silence. "I'm sure we'd all like to thank the reverend Billy Swagger for those inspiring words which we all enjoyed," she said. "Let's all give him a big clap... That's enough! That's enough, I say. We have work to do! It's time for morning lessons. I want you to all file out of this assembly hall in an orderly manner, starting with year 11."

Lavinia merged with her year group, streaming along the corridor towards her geography lesson – flat earth geography taught by a gloomy scripture teacher who sat at his desk and spoke in a low mumble while the class chatted among themselves and exchanged notes and missiles. A prefect brushed past her, wielding a notebook.

"Lavinia Machin?"

Several heads turned to observe her reaction.

"Miss Cattermole is waiting for you in the counselling room."

The prefect walked ahead, directing her to follow. Good news, she thought. Miss Cattermole could tell her what had happened to the boy. Catherine Cattermole doubled as guidance counsellor and PE teacher. Lavinia remembered that Josh was supposed to be good at PE. That must be why the Cat Lady took such an interest in him.

Miss Cattermole waited at her open office door, a tall athletic lady in designer jeans. She wore a pink embroidered top, and pearl earrings dangled beneath her short fair hair. "Why, Lavinia! Lavinia Machin, isn't it?" she said in a half-whisper. She came up close, with a twinkle in her eyes and a fresh smell of scent. "It's really nice to see you," she murmured. "I have heard so much about you, but I believe this is the first time we've met. Come and take a seat. No, not over there. Come and sit beside me on the couch."

Apart from a small table and two chairs, the couch, which was long, white and luxurious, took up an entire wall of the room. The Cat Lady leaned towards her so that their shoulders were almost touching and gave her another confiding smile, fragrant with empathy.

"So, Lavinia, I know how you must be feeling," she said. "How are you managing to cope with it all?"

"All right," she said.

"All right." The Cat Lady cradled her words as if they were precious. "It must be hard having such a famous father."

"Stepfather," Lavinia corrected her.

The Cat Lady gave her a quick look of understanding. "Of course; stepfather! It's not the same, is it? I expect there must be times when you feel quite rebellious?" She gave a little giggle of admiration and gazed into her eyes, adding "I mean over things like going to church on Sundays?"

"Twice," said Lavinia, nodding. The Cat Lady understood her. Of course she felt rebellious! Who wouldn't?

"Except you don't always go, do you?"

Lavinia felt a sudden tension in her shoulders. Why did she ask that question? Any moment now they would talk about the boy. She saw those teasing eyes observing her intently. "What makes you think that?" she asked, leaning back a little.

"I was thinking about this afternoon."

She knew. The Cat Lady knew! But then, if she was helping Josh escape, it didn't matter.

Lavinia hesitated. She decided to play dumb for the moment. "I was there, in the church. Maybe you just didn't see me."

"Oh really?"

It was obvious that the Cat Lady didn't believe her. Lavinia watched in dismay as she rose from her chair and walked over to her desk. Lavinia felt a sudden withdrawal of affection. The Cat Lady fiddled in her drawer, took out some papers and began taking notes as if she no longer existed. There was something about her that compelled Lavinia to try and regain her approval. "How is your aunt?" she asked.

"I don't have an aunt," said the Cat Lady. Her voice was soft and gentle again.

Lavinia stared in horror.

"You've been speaking with the boy, haven't you?" said the Cat Lady. She came and sat beside her again on the couch, this time sitting a little closer. "We are all so worried about the boy. We don't know where he is."

Lavinia leaned away from her perfumed presence and her probing, catlike eyes. "But I thought you agreed to meet him," she said.

"Oh, but I did! I did! But now I don't know where he is!"

"Oh dear!" exclaimed Lavinia, hiding her relief.

"Oh dear!" The Cat Lady echoed her words in affectionate mockery. "So where do you think he can have gone? We have to find him for his own safety." She took out her diary, prepared to make notes.

"What will you do when you find him?" asked Lavinia.

"Make sure he's safe," said the Cat Lady, ripping out the page and tossing it in the bin. She got up and sat behind her desk. "Now Lavinia, I want you to help us," she said, poised to reopen her diary. "Where do you think he can have gone?"

Lavinia shrugged. "I dunno," she said. "He said you were going to pick him up."

The Cat Lady put down her pen. "But we both know that didn't happen. You have to do better than that, Lavinia!"

"He could have gone to the village."

Instantly, the Cat Lady returned to the couch. "The village. Do you think we should try the village? Does he know anyone in the village? I mean, you were the last person to see him."

"I dunno, but he might need to go the shops, to buy food for instance."

The Cat Lady nodded. Her eyes had lost their friendliness. "Now, Lavinia, we know he's heading for Amaryllis. I want the truth now. I want to know where he is. His safety is important to us."

"But I don't know the truth!"

Suddenly, she felt the grip of the Cat Lady's arms pinning her to the couch. "Relax, Lavinia. There's nothing to be afraid of.

You must know where he is. You have to tell me." Her voice was soothing but her eyes were catlike.

Lavinia gave a faint smile. Teachers didn't grab you unless they'd lost control. Jerking herself out of her grasp, she stood up. "Don't touch me," she said in her calmest manner. "The truth is you don't know where the boy is and neither do I, because you've lost him. Yes, lost him!"

"But that's not my fault!" wailed the Cat Lady.

"Good excuse! That's what I'll tell my stepdad when I get home. You're working for him, aren't you? And in return, I expect he gives you nice things."

In spite of herself, the Cat Lady looked down at the diamond brooch on her chest. "He trusts me," she said. She gave her hair a little shake and held her head up high.

"And now you've lost that boy; but I'll tell him it wasn't your fault. I'm sure he'll love that. He's always so understanding, don't you find?"

"Maybe it would be best if you didn't say anything," said the Cat Lady sweetly.

"Maybe," agreed Lavinia, with her hand on the doorknob, returning the Cat Lady's smile. "Who knows?"

CHAPTER SIX

A s soon as they left the fort behind them, Josh volunteered
to steer Bertie's speed boat across the open sea. You just
had to hold the wheel steady and tune your speed to the strength
of the waves so that they didn't swamp the boat or throw it off
course. It didn't feel like travelling through water – more like
thumping over floorboards; on and on and on through the dark
mist until your arms ached and your clothes got soaked. His
stepdad would have loved to be on this boat, he thought. Ever
since they came to this island, he'd hired a boat at weekends to
go fishing or simply explore the coastline. That's how Josh had
learnt to hold the tiller. His stepdad had taught him to sail too.

He eased his hands on the tiller and looked around him. On
his left, Megs lay flat out on the bench that ran along the sides,
resting on a bed of old clothes, her body sliding up and down
with the motion of the boat. Bertie sat facing Josh in the bows,
laughing at the buffeting of the waves.

"If you look over to starboard," Bertie shouted above the
spray, "you can just see the island of Discovery. Do you see it?
Josh, Megs?"

"I thought we were heading for Crown Colony!" Josh cried.
He slumped at the tiller and turned off the engine, letting the
boat drift. Discovery Island had no heliport. He'd never get to

Amaryllis at this rate. In the sudden stillness, he listened to the waves lapping against the sides of the boat and felt the dark immensity of the ocean leading him further and further away from his destination.

"Sorry! Change of plan!" Bertie shouted. "Discovery's nearer. Didn't you see those helicopters passing over the fort? They know where we are heading. We'll get to Crown Colony eventually but not till long after midnight. We'll just have to slip in there quietly when they've given up the chase."

Josh knew Bertie was right, but it didn't make him any less miserable. He slackened speed and gazed ahead at the shadowy outlines of Discovery Island. He could see the cliffs and what looked like a harbour to the south east ringed with twinkling lights.

Bertie blinked and rubbed his eyes. "Sorry, Josh," he said. "Look, I'll take over for a bit if you want a rest."

Josh took the hint. "I'm ok." He engaged the engine again and redirected the boat towards the shore. "How far is it?" he asked.

"Not far at all!" cried Bertie. "Another ten minutes, by my reckoning."

Josh turned the engine up to maximum speed and struggled to maintain the boat on course as it bumped up and down through the waves. They hadn't lost much time after all. Another ten minutes and they'd be up and away again, on course for Crown Colony.

"Look, no hurry, Josh," Bertie called out. His arms were clutching the railings.

Josh relaxed the speed a little and they travelled on in silence for a bit. It was difficult to talk above the roar of the motor and the crash of sea spray whooshing over the deck. There was another noise too that Josh gradually became aware of; an insistent background hum, like the drone of a trapped bluebottle, coming from far away in the skies behind him.

"What's that sound?" he called out.

Bertie pointed upwards. "A helicopter!" he shouted.

"Has it seen us?"

"Not yet!" Bertie stood, with his back to the railings, impervious to the spray. "It would be here in no time if it had spotted us. Steer a course to starboard; ten degrees. Can you see those lights over there?"

"Is that the harbour?"

"Yes, Greystones. It's less than a mile away. Full throttle now and keep altering your course. With any luck, we'll reach land before – Damn! It's seen us!"

The hum became a throbbing roar.

Josh turned and saw the helicopter falling out of the night sky and speeding towards the boat. He changed course abruptly, aiming away from the harbour lights. Too late. It had loomed so close now that he could see the pilot, aiming his machine directly at them. A pinging sound like heavy rain churned up the water in a wide circle around them.

"Alter course!" cried Bertie. "Before he hits us!"

Josh swung the tiller round as far as he dared without capsizing the boat and shut his eyes to protect himself from the spray. When he opened them again, the noise had gone. "What happened?" he asked, staring up at the sky. He saw the helicopter making an upward arc in preparation for its next descent.

"He overshot his mark!" cried Bertie. "But he'll be back again in a minute. Josh! Help me lower the dinghy! Quickly, before he gets close enough to see us. We have to get to the cover of those rocks. And Megs! Collect our baggage. All of it! Get ready to load it on board. That's my girl! Jump on board first. Try to hold it steady. Now!"

Bertie handed Josh the rope attached to the dinghy. "Right, Josh. I'm next because you're lighter than me. I want you to set the boat on a different course at full speed and then jump. Got it? Good. He's turning again. Now!"

Josh jumped just in time and scrambled into the dinghy before the speed boat shot away from them. It drifted to a standstill a few feet away from the dinghy, but by this time Bertie had the oars in his hands and had built up enough momentum to increase the distance from the speed boat, steering away from the bright lights of the harbour towards the dark shelter of the rocks.

The helicopter dropped out of the sky like an angry gannet, spewing bullets all around the boat.

"He's missed it!" cried Bertie. "He'll have to make another turn at this rate."

"It only takes one bullet," Josh observed. "Look! It's tilting in the water."

Whoosh! A column of flames and thick black smoke shot upwards from the fuel tank. The boat bobbed up and down in the water for a few seconds, then waves rushed in and turned it on its side. They sat and watched it sink in a widening circle of bubbles, leaving nothing but a few charred remnants floating on the waves.

They waited in the shadow of the rocks until the helicopter did a victory wave and turned away, heading towards its base on Colony Island.

"I'm sorry about your boat," said Josh quietly, thinking it was mainly for his sake that Bertie had just lost his most precious possession.

Bertie shrugged. "We're alive; that's what counts at the moment," he said. "And with a bit of luck we'll soon all be safely in Crown Colony."

They picked their way in a straggling line across the rocks towards the harbour. They found Greystones empty of life at this time of night, but plenty of blue fishing dories bobbed at anchor in the harbour.

"Pick one without a name and – if possible – with provisions and a spare can of petrol," Bertie called out as Josh raced ahead along the rickety landing bay. "I feel bad about this," he muttered, panting along behind him. "We'll have to make it up to the owners somehow, once this is all over."

Josh settled on a battered blue fishing dory, its deck littered with fish scales and tarry rope. "I'll take the helm," he said, as they all stumbled on board. "I've been on boats like this before. Besides, I don't feel tired at the moment. Just show me the direction and I'll be fine."

Stars twinkled in the night sky as they left the harbour behind them. The wind had dropped and they headed south on the flat, empty sea.

"Wake me when you've had enough," said Bertie. "I'll cook you all breakfast as soon as it gets light. We should reach Crown Colony before midday." He went over and sat propped against the sides of the hatchway, his head nodding forward as he drifted off to sleep.

Josh looked up from the wheel to see Megs standing beside him, with a thick bundle in her arms. "I don't need this," she said, draping the coat over his shoulders. "I'm going down to the cabin for a kip."

"Thanks, Megs, but it's cold in the cabin. I'm really okay."

"Don't talk posh," she said crossly. "Just wear it." She turned her back on him so that he couldn't see her expression as she hurried towards the hatchway.

He sat there for a few moments, feeling the warmth of the coat round his shoulders and thinking warm thoughts about Megs. She might have a sharp tongue, but he'd rather have her by his side in a crisis than some of the kids he knew at school. He opened and closed his eyes a few times, in an effort to keep awake.

"Are you all right there?" called Bertie from the hatchway.

"I'm fine, thanks," said Josh. "Do you think they know where we are now?"

Bertie stared back across the ocean. "They'll think you went down with that speed boat," he said "but, when the owner reports his boat missing, they'll probably guess it's us." He grinned. "We're safe for the moment! When we reach Crown Colony, that's when we've got to worry."

Josh checked his direction and adjusted the wheel a fraction. He needed time to think this out. Maybe Bertie could help him. He seemed like someone you could trust for advice. "Do you know Magnus Maxtrader?" he asked.

"Know him or know of him? Everyone knows about Magnus Maxtrader."

Josh hesitated. "It's just that I've got to give him a message," he said.

Bertie came over and sat beside him. "Is there something you're not telling me?" he asked.

Josh spoke in a rush. "Lavinia came to my house, just this morning," he said, "Machin's stepdaughter. "She thinks her mum's in danger, and she wants Maxtrader to rescue her. And she's offered to help me rescue my parents and…."

Bertie sat and thought about what Josh had told him. "Lavinia!" he exclaimed. "And she wants you to rescue her mum but not herself? And she's Machin's stepdaughter. I'd say you've got a useful ally there …if she's telling the truth." He went into another long silence. "In any case," he said at last. "It gives us an introduction to Magnus Maxtrader – if we can tell him we have a message from his granddaughter, he's bound to listen, and there's no telling how much he may be able to help us."

He nodded and wandered back to his place at the hatchway, rested his head on a coil of old rope and closed his eyes. In a moment Josh could hear him snoring.

Josh sat at the wheel and stared with unseeing eyes at his future. His fingers closed round the stone, drawing comfort from its warmth. 'Choices.' He thought again of that dry voice telling him not to whinge; hardly the kind of help you expected from the Guardian's stone. But he felt proud of making that cliff jump and leading the way down the well. He wished his mother had been there at those moments. She looked so slim and fragile, but she was brave herself and she'd always encouraged him to take risks. She'd shown him how to dive from high rocks. She'd have been proud of him making that cliff jump.

He kept one hand firmly on the wheel, scared of being driven off course. He thought again about that girl. He had to speak to her grandfather. But Magnus Maxtrader was an important man. Would he speak to him? He must do if he knew his daughter stood in danger. But what then? Would Lavinia keep her side of the bargain? Would she get his parents released from gaol? "I just have to trust her," he muttered. "There's no other way."

He looked round to find Bertie standing behind him at the wheel. How long had he been there?

"Talking to yourself?" asked Bertie. "You must be tired." He held a steadying hand on the wheel. "I've left some cooked food for you down there," he said. "Lucky we found a boat so stocked with provisions, though I feel bad about stealing them. Go on! There's an extra space in the cabin. Go down and get some sleep."

Josh stumbled down the steps to the cabin and threw himself onto the bottom bunk. His eyes felt leaden and he wanted to drift into a deep, dark sleep. But, even as he slept, the blood thundered in his temples and wouldn't allow him to sink into oblivion. Less than a day had passed since he last saw his parents. Less than a day! His mind raced through a tunnel of darkness, picking out recent memories, like posters affixed to the walls. He was standing outside his kitchen window, bouncing a rubber ball against a wall. He heard the tinkle of glass but, when he looked again, it wasn't glass but a shower of bullets that pinged in the water all around him. He was in a boat and one of the bullets hit the fuel tank and lit up the night sky in a puff of brilliant colours. Then the colours falling from the sky became small, round silver balls and the hideously deranged figure of Reginald Machin caught one of them and started bouncing it against the wall beneath Josh's kitchen window, threatening to blow up the world.

Josh blinked, rubbed his eyes and sat up. For a moment he felt afraid. Then he remembered he was on a boat among friends heading for Crown Colony and he lay back and listened to the gentle rocking movement of the boat on a flat sea and drifted into a deeper sleep.

CHAPTER SEVEN

The sun shone brightly overhead when Josh climbed back on deck. The boat rode at anchor at the edge of a cluster of fishing vessels in a noisy, crowded harbour. Inland, above the quay, white skyscrapers loomed like icebergs in the smoky haze. His eyes returned to the empty deck. How long had he been asleep? The others must have gone on shore. He found a seat on Bertie's coil of old rope and stared in wonder at Paradise City, the capital of Crown Colony and the largest city he'd ever seen.

But as he stared, masts and sails and buildings and city lights began to wobble before his eyes and flicker in the haze. He began to feel dizzy. He squeezed his eyes shut and reached for his stone but it didn't respond. He broke into a sweat and his head began to throb. His lifeline had gone.

He clenched his fists and tried to think. It didn't happen very often but he knew when a fit was coming on. He would reach for his stone and the dizziness would slowly wash away. But this was no ordinary fit. He felt wide awake and his dangerous mission burned inside his mind. But he didn't know where to turn. Something told him he had to make sense of his thoughts before he could wring sense out of the stone. He had to concentrate, focus all his thoughts into a single idea, bright and hard as a diamond in the dark. Crown Colony, Amaryllis, his

parents in prison, his enemies waiting on shore, Lavinia, Magnus
Maxtrader…Lavinia!

The stone in his hand began to glow. He clutched it and felt
his headache drain away. That girl held the key to his questions.
He had to find her with his stone. As soon as he said this to
himself, he felt liberated; free as a butterfly breaking out of its
dark web into a different world.

The stone was fully open now and what he was witnessing
seemed much larger and more lifelike than the events on the tiny
screen. The deck beneath his feet had become a red carpet. He
scuffed it with his soiled boots but they didn't leave a mark. That
girl brushed past him. She wore the same long black skirt and
white embroidered blouse as when she stopped at his house. But
she didn't see him. Just to make sure, he coughed but she didn't
turn round. He followed her along a wide, red-carpeted corridor,
moistening his fingers and touching one wall as he went past. No
moisture appeared on the wall. He felt transported to another
place where he could see without being seen.

Like a shadow, he followed in her footsteps, keeping a few
paces behind. Even from behind she looked different from the
girl that had stopped at his house. She looked nervous, as if she
were meeting someone important. She held her head up high and
stopped at the half-open door at the end of the corridor to do up
the top button of her blouse.

*On the far side of a large, lighted room, the tall figure of
Reginald Machin sat in a high-backed chair at the centre of a
long table. Four guards in smart blue uniforms stood at attention
behind his chair, projecting silent menace. Waiters in white coats
hurried past them, holding up steaming dishes loaded on silver
trays. Broad-shouldered and alert, Machin gazed round the
room with his penetrating blue eyes and smiled, like the
handsome politician Josh had seen on the telescreen. But there
was something dangerously unhinged about his smile. And from*

time to time his right eye twitched, and he twiddled his fork, as if he wanted to stab it into the nearest face.

Lavinia sat beside her mother in the centre, facing her stepdad. A line of secretaries lined up behind Machin's chair with documents for him to sign. They smiled when he smiled and gave a nod each time he spoke, like puppets jerking up and down on strings. He could even hear them speak.

While Machin turned to snatch another document from an outstretched hand, Josh heard Lavinia whisper in her mother's ear, "Why's he wearing a black tie?"

"I don't know," her mother whispered back, holding a napkin to her mouth, "probably in mourning for someone he's killed." Her mother looked slim and elegant, with short golden hair and a face that would look good on the telescreen. She sat prodding her breakfast around her plate with pale, sad eyes.

Machin glanced up from his documents and dismissed his last secretary with a wave of the hand.

"Why, if it isn't Slug!" he called out across the table.

Her mum raised a weak protest. "Her name's Lavinia!"

Josh saw Lavinia give her mum's hand a squeeze of support under the table.

Machin answered with another twitch and a twisted smile. "She doesn't mind me calling her Slug," he said, raising his eyebrows in fake surprise. "You don't mind, do you, Slug?"

"Of course I don't mind, Dad," she said. Her voice sounded sugary and false.

Her stepdad frowned. His eye started to twitch again. "Good," he said. "I expect you were wondering why I was wearing black today. You see, I have to attend a funeral. It's the right thing to do." He smiled and repeated himself. "Yes, it's the right thing to do. I do like that turn of phrase. You don't have to explain why. It's the answer to everything!"

"Yes, Dad. Is it someone we know?"

"Percy...Percy something or other. The head of the opposition. The name's gone right out of my head. Your mother would know. She seemed quite fond of him."

"Percy Gibson," her mum said; "one of the few honest men in politics."

"A pirate," he muttered. "There are still too many pirates in high positions. That's something we'll have to change."

"How did he die?" asked her mum, without looking up.

"I'm told he was trying to fly," he said, studying his fingernails. "Not an easy act to perform at his age; not at any age, I suppose – especially from a fifth-floor window."

"He wanted to have you impeached," her mum persisted.

"Well, I'm a forgiving man. That's why I shall attend his funeral. I hope you'll come too, Slug."

"Her name's Lavinia," her mum almost shouted across the table.

"You don't mind being called Slug, do you, Slug?" he asked Lavinia again, toying with his fork.

For a moment, Lavinia's mask seemed to slip. She looked down at her arms as if to say, "Yes, I'm fat. I know that's what you mean."

"Your mother's not a slug," he went on. He leant back in his chair, his eyes dancing with mischief. "No, she rather reminds me of a goose, with that long neck and prominent beak and those wide eyes."

Her mother gave him a sad stare. "I'm surprised you forgot to mention the golden egg."

Lavinia quietly put down her knife and fork. Her stepdad had gone very cold. "Ah, the Maxtrader fortune," he said in a soft voice, adding with a chuckle, "Daddy's money! I don't know where I'd be without it."

Machin's hand went to the red flower in his buttonhole.

Lavinia gave a prim little cough. "Daddy, dear," she asked. "What's that flower? I've never seen a flower like that before."

Machin took the flower from his buttonhole and held it in the palm of his hand. "How observant of you, my dear Slug!" he said. "This is 'oblivia preciosa', or the 'forget me flower,' to give its common name. It only grows on the other side of the island – or the other side of the world, if my dear friends in the Flat Earth Church are to be believed. It's amazing how some of our more enterprising citizens have managed to get their hands on it! The juice of this flower makes a very effective sleeping pill. Wasn't it a pirate, Prince Rupert the Rotten, who first discovered its uses? He wanted to poison our drinking water with it when the first colonists arrived on the island. Poor Rupert! Right idea, wrong century! My scientists are working on a way of refining this juice still further until it can be used as a weapon. And with this weapon at my disposal" – he stabbed a look of malice at her mum – "I won't be needing Daddy's money for much longer."

"If there's any left," her mum said, staring at her empty plate.

Machin smiled and looked around the room, raising his voice to let his audience into the conversation. "We need money," he said. "We have to build up our defences. That's why more than half the country voted for me."

"The colonist half."

"Yes, that's more than half. I promised to tackle unemployment. Now they've all got jobs."

"The colonists have got jobs; mostly jobs we don't need. We've suddenly got thousands of soldiers, policemen, prison warders. When my father learns what's happened to all his profits, he's going to cut off our funds. What will you do then?"

Machin turned away. His mocking eyes returned to Lavinia's mother. Then he reached over and ran a finger down the side of her neck. "But Daddy's not going to know, is he?" he whispered – "not if we all know what's good for us."

Her mum gave a weak shrug. "I no longer know what you are thinking half the time!"

He leant back and smiled. "I am thinking about what you just told me, my silly goose" he said. "We are wasting too much money on security. Too many useless mouths to feed; there must be another way." He fingered the flower in his buttonhole.

"So you will release some of your prisoners? They are mostly pirates who have committed no crime apart from being poor and unemployed."

Machin stabbed his fork into the table. "Look!" he shouted, "You have no idea what you are talking about! Half the people on this island are pirates; the lazy half, if the truth were told. I promised to make this island safe for honest colonists to live in. We can build a new society, just as in the old days when men were men. We should have done this years ago when we first arrived on this island."

Silence. Josh could hear the steady ticking of the clock on the wall. He could see from the way that Lavinia gripped her mother's arm that she supported her mother. And he could see from the look on that maniac's face that her mother's life hung by a thread. But did she really need to cosy up to her stepdad like that?

"When are you going to stop all this?" her mum asked.

"Stop what?"

"How many pirates are in prison, or dead for that matter, since you took over?"

"I can't possibly answer that question. I was never any good at mathematics. After I get past a hundred, my calculations go a bit wobbly."

Her mum sighed and tried another tack. "What about all the money you waste on your CP and your odious Chief of Police? Saintly-Smith? That's his name, isn't it? Have you ever thought that, by giving so much power to a man like that, there'll come a time when he uses it against you?"

A knocking could be heard at the door behind Machin's chair. "Maybe you'd like to say that to his face?" he said. "Don't let me stop you."

Suddenly Lavinia sat up straight and fixed her stepdad with her clear blue eyes and said, "Daddy!"

"Yes, Slug?"

"Mum's right, you know."

He raised his eyebrows in amusement.

"Saintly needs watching," she urged. "They all do. Why don't you let me help?"

Machin licked his lips, as if to see how the idea tasted and gave a mocking laugh. "You, Slug?" he asked. "How could my poor little Slug be any use to me in a grown-up world?"

Her mum turned to her in shock. "For goodness' sake, Lavinia, have you taken leave of your senses?"

Lavinia ignored her. She leant towards her stepdad, hands on the table, and spoke to him with honest, pleading eyes. "You need someone you can trust, Daddy," she said. "That's all. I may be young but I've got eyes and ears and no one will suspect me. I can report what they say when you're out of the room, and I can make tea for everyone and I can type and–"

Her mother banged her plate on the table and hurried out of the room.

Josh felt his sympathies swing from Lavinia to her mother. He remembered the confident girl who'd barged into his house and poured scorn on her stepdad and his associates. Now she just soaked up his insults and wanted to help him. He felt his trust in her slipping away. He could hardly bear to watch her.

He saw the effect she had on her stepdad. He seemed to be seeing her for the first time and he licked his lips with satisfaction. "Well, Slug, I do believe…" He hesitated. "Saintly's still waiting. You might as well start by letting him in."

A heavy presence entered the room.

Machin gestured to the Specials who quickly made their exits. "Come and join us, Saintly," he said. "You never know who might be listening."

"I make it my business to know," said Saintly in a gravelly voice, staring around him like an ex-criminal, wary of enemies lurking in doorways, "I have a nose for it."

He pointed to his nose and winked. His face looked weathered and bruised: the face of a born survivor.

"Well, Saintly. What's the news on the fugitives?"

Saintly gave a sideways glance at Lavinia, eyebrows raised.

"Ah, Saintly, meet my stepdaughter, Lavinia. I've taken her on as my apprentice."

"Charmed to meet you, I'm sure." He came round and sat down heavily in the chair beside her, muscles bulging through his black leather jacket. A rich odour of garlic and aftershave filled the room.

Machin tapped the table. "I want to know about the boy."

Josh grasped the sides of his seat. How could they sit there and not see him, a shadow in their midst?

"Do you have a picture of him?" asked Lavinia, risking her stepdad's anger.

"What are you talking about?" he shouted. "You are here as a silent witness. One more word and I will ask you to leave the room."

"I am here to help you, Daddy," she said patiently. "If we have to track down this boy, I need to know what he looks like. What happens if they fob you off with the wrong boy? You wouldn't know without his picture."

Her stepdad stared at her for a moment and gave a slow nod of acceptance.

Saintly fished in his jacket and handed her a stained and creased photograph. "That's him," he growled. "The name's Josh. You can keep it if you want." He turned to her stepdad.

"We spotted him escaping to Discovery Island," he said. "We managed to blow up the boat, but I soon smelt something fishy going on there." He pointed to his nose again, as proof of his criminal instincts, and said, "Sure enough, a fishing vessel's

been reported missing. He must be in Crown Colony by now. Don't worry. We'll nail him as soon as he tries to land."

"What's so important about this boy?" asked Lavinia. Her stepdad looked ready to explode so she quickly explained, "I need to know, you see. I can't be any use to you unless you put me in the picture."

Machin opened and closed his mouth a few times before Saintly forestalled him. "She's a bright kid, eh? I reckon I were a bit like that when I started my career," he said. He turned to Lavinia and explained, "It's all in that holy book them pirates read – the Piratica. This boy's meant to be some kind of saviour, see. Sooner we can wipe him out the better, if you ask me."

"But you haven't succeeded, have you?" complained her stepdad.

"We will, sir, we will."

"Well, find that boat. How is our other project going?"

Saintly's voice descended to a husky croak. "The factory," he said, "is going to plan, sir, according to Dr Fleck."

Machin cast his eyes to the ceiling and seemed to ponder for a moment. "Ah, yes! That factory," he said with a taunting smile. "It's beyond the mist. According to your religion, that's beyond the edge of the world. Do correct me if I'm wrong, Saintly."

Saintly squirmed in his chair. "I wouldn't know about that, sir," he said.

"You haven't noticed all those barges – all that steel and cement – all that slave labour – heading past the northwest headland – your own work force?"

"No, sir. Don't tempt my faith, sir."

"Well, if ignorance is bliss, you must be in ecstasy."

"Where's that, sir?"

Machin sighed. "Never mind, Saintly," he said. "Stick to what you're good at – religion and slitting throats. Tell me about our weapon."

"Fleck says that the oblivion flower will be ready for harvesting in a few days. We've already picked a few samples and our scientists have distilled the juice to a high level of concentration; pirate scientists, of course. At least we know that the weapon works."

"How's that, then?"

"Every time one of them lets a tiny drop of the concentrated solution fall on his clothes, the man's a complete vegetable. He can't remember a thing."

Machin didn't look impressed. "Well, we are all a bit forgetful, sometimes," he said.

"You don't get my meaning, sir. Oblivion means what it says; total loss of memory. Without memory, we can't even eat, sleep or get up in the morning."

"And what about the means of delivery?"

"Ah! That's what we're working on, sir. Fleck's thinking of adding the solution to a crop spray. But he's also working on a bomb. We'll have to try out the spray on a few prisoners first to make sure we get the quantities just right. After that, we can pick off our enemies at random, sir."

"That's very gratifying," said Reginald Machin, "What do you think, Lavinia?"

"It all sounds wonderfully exciting!" she said.

Josh had heard enough. He had to get out of there fast. He thought of his parents sitting in that prison. Bertie had told him they'd be safe for the moment, but what exactly did 'safe' mean when that maniac was bent on genocide? They had to get to Amaryllis quickly and get help, before that maniac perfected his weapon. Then nobody would be safe!

CHAPTER EIGHT

J osh had the sensation of falling through space. When he came to, he found he'd bashed the back of his head on a plank. He'd been there! He'd been in a different world where he could see and hear without being seen, a hidden camera in a far-off room.

He looked at the cluster of fishing vessels bobbing up and down in the harbour and Paradise City looming through the mist. It was nearly midday. The others had been gone a long time. Didn't they know it was dangerous to step on shore?

His mind kept jumping back to that madman and the red 'forget-me' flower in his buttonhole. He'd never expected that flower to be so thick and velvety; quite different from the blue 'forget-me-not' to which it was supposed to be related. If every plant had a cluster of flowers like this, that man could spray the juice everywhere. And in a few days, the crop would be ready for harvesting. He had to be stopped before then.

Just then, Josh thought he heard a woman's voice calling from the water and a fisherman from one of the neighbouring boats shouting out a reply. Several voices joined in but none of them sounded like Bertie or Megs. They had to be back soon! He walked over to the side of the boat and scanned the harbour. You couldn't see much through the mist and it would've been hard anyway to pick out his friends from the crowd swarming around the waterfront. He looked for their rubber dinghy but there were hundreds of similar dinghies moored on jetties along the quayside.

"Josh Flagsmith!"

Someone had just shouted out his name. The owner of a nearby fishing dory leaned over the side of his boat and pointed at something he'd spotted in the water.

"There's a lady asking for a boy called Josh Flagsmith," the man called out. "Is that you?"

Josh nodded. He ran to the side of the dory and saw a solitary figure standing up in a rowing boat, waving vigorously enough to risk toppling into the water.

"It's a lady," the fisherman called out. "I think she's asking for help."

Josh took a closer look. "Miss Cattermole!" he cried. "Be careful! The water's quite choppy out there. Sit down and I'll help you on board."

He manoeuvred the boat slowly in her direction. He wondered how someone as nimble as Miss Cattermole could be silly enough to stand up in a rowing boat. So, she'd managed to come after all! Maybe she knew some quicker way of getting them to Amaryllis! But why hadn't she met him at the house? Bertie hadn't wanted to explain.

He helped her attach her boat to the dory and clamber aboard, half soaked with sea spray, overjoyed to be rescued 'so unexpectedly'. She wore jeans and a frilly white blouse and carried a rucksack which she 'was only too glad' for Josh to stow below deck. "Thank you so much!" she purred in his ear as he came back with a blanket to drape round her shoulders. "It was wonderful how I managed to catch up with you at last," she said. "For a time I thought I'd never find you again. I don't know what your parents would think of me then!" Her eyes widened as she said it.

"How did you manage to get off school?" asked Josh. He'd always admired her so much. Now he felt the disappointment of knowing he'd grown out of her; he didn't quite know why.

"Well, you see, Josh" she said, resting her fathomless eyes on his face. "I've been given compassionate leave for a few days. My aunt lives in Crown Colony and I got news that she'd been taken ill."

"Is that why you couldn't come to pick me up?"

Her eyes flickered away from him. "I did come," she said, patting her hair down, "but I was too late." Her eyes widened again. "Still, it's good to see how wonderfully you've managed in my absence," she said. "I always knew you would." She paused and a tear the size of a pearl formed in the corner of one eye. "My aunt died yesterday," she added in a quiet voice.

"I'm very sorry," said Josh. He did feel sorry for the Cat Lady but he couldn't help being glad of an excuse not to stop for too long in Crown Colony

She gave him another look of bright-eyed empathy and said, "It's all right, Josh. You didn't know. One just has to get over these things." She gave a little toss of her head, letting her hair fly upwards and fall back into place. "Anyway, that's not really why I came out here. I've come to take you to Amaryllis. I–" She stopped and cupped a delicate hand to her ear. "Gosh!" she cried, "it sounds as if your friends are returning."

He smiled as he listened to Megs' high-pitched chatter and Bertie cursing as he struggled to attach the dinghy to the side of the dory. But he detected something nervous and jerky in the Cat Lady's reaction. Her eyes darted in the direction of the sound, then to the other side of the dory where her boat was moored. She stood up and checked her watch. "And the funeral is in half an hour," she said, pointing to her clothes. "And I haven't even got changed." She gave him a fond glance, whispering in his ear, "Look, we'll meet up very soon." Then her eyes flickered away again and she hurried to the side of the boat, murmuring over her shoulder, "I'm staying just across the water. We'll meet soon. But I must fly now–" As she spoke, she already had one foot over the side of the boat. And in a few deft movements, she settled into her little rowing boat, revved up the engine with one hand and gave a backward wave with the other as she steered a course towards the shore.

"Wait a minute!" cried Josh, "You've forgotten your rucksack! Miss Cattermole! Wait!"

Too late; she couldn't hear him.

He turned and saw Megs clambering on board. Bertie got on next and hurried past him, saying "I'll explain in a moment." He took a quick look round the deck, then darted down the hatchway.

"We may have a problem," said Bertie, as he climbed back on deck, holding the Cat Lady's rucksack in one hand.

"She's working for them," said Megs, scowling at Bertie. "Why don't you just say it?"

Bertie didn't answer.

Josh watched open-mouthed as he swung the bag behind his head and tossed it like a frisbee into the sea. "Now steer a course back towards the harbour," he told Josh – "fast as you can!"

Nobody moved.

"Before it explodes," he added.

Josh stared unbelieving out to sea.

"She let you down, didn't she?" said Megs, clutching his arm. "I only met her once. I knew she was a bit of a fake, but there you go."

"There I go where?" he thought, staring at the spot where the rucksack had made its final splash. Had she really meant to kill him? He stared at the sudden turbulence in the water. The aftershock created a small tidal wave which rocked the whole cluster of fishing boats and sent water splashing across their decks. Why would she want to do that to him? He shook his head in disbelief.

Josh scanned the harbour for a sight of the Cat Lady. He spotted her eventually, mooring her boat and clambering onto the quay. "How did you know?" he asked Bertie.

"I hacked into Machin's e-mails," said Bertie. "There's a small group of us working for the opposition – Sandy's dad is one of us. Machin gets a lot of correspondence from a lady who signs herself 'cat'. It could only be her. That's why we sent Sandy to pick you up. Remember?"

"She's really working for Machin?"

"Yes."

"So all that bit about the funeral; I suppose that was a lie?"

"Probably. It hardly matters, does it? She still found time to row out here and try to blow you out of the water."

"How did she find the boat?"

"It wouldn't take Machin's spies long to find out that a boat had gone missing. I expect they've got people on the quayside – or even in one of those boats – waiting to pick you up."

"Do you think they'd do that?"

"Pick you up? Not in broad daylight; Crown Colony's not too keen on people from other islands breaking the law in its own backyard. Still, we'd be safer back among those fishing boats. They're all pirates in those boats and you're a bit of a local hero now."

Josh realised it was time to drop anchor. They'd already come a little too close to the shore for comfort. "How do they know about me?" he asked.

Bertie went and sat on his coil of old rope. "We met a group of fishermen on shore," he said. "We told them all about you. Some of them are from Colony Island. They're not going back there in a hurry."

Josh took a second look at the cluster of fishing vessels surrounding them. Pirates appeared on deck and cheered and waved their flags. Josh waved back and felt a thrill of acceptance. He tried hard to stop thinking about the Cat Lady.

He left the tiller and went over to talk to Bertie. "You and Megs have been gone all morning," he said. "What took you so long?"

Bertie gave a satisfied smile. He reached into his jacket and hauled out a wad of notes with figures scribbled in neat rows on every page. "I have a friend who's working for Squabble and Dick. That's Maxtrader's accountants," he said. "Except, they're not just working for Maxtrader. They're working for Machin." He pointed to his notes. "My friend is a bit of a hacker too. He feeds me information from time to time. Do you know what he's discovered?"

"Machin's run out of funds?"

"Maxtrader's funds, yes. How did you guess?

"I didn't exactly guess. I saw it! Listen. I'll try and explain."

Bertie sat back and listened while Josh told him everything he'd seen and heard in Machin's dining-room.

"Can you do that any time you want?" he asked, "I can't say I envy you. It must be a frightening experience."

"It's scary," Josh said. "But it's only happened twice and I don't know if it will happen again."

"You seem worried about something," Bertie observed. "Does that have something to do with what you saw through your stone?"

"Well, you know Machin's stepdaughter?"

"Lavinia?"

"Yes. I don't know if I can trust her."

Bertie patted the coil of old rope. "Look, sit down and tell me about it. There's room for both of us," he said. "Go over what you saw."

"Well, she came to my house."

"I know. That's in her favour. She'd have been in trouble if she'd been caught."

"And she gave me a letter to give to her grandfather."

"I know. That shows she trusts you and she's prepared to take a risk to save her mother."

"I know, but after that–"

Bertie gave him a penetrating stare. "What do you mean 'after that'?" he asked. "In your vision?"

"Yes. She agreed with everything Machin said. She even offered to work for him!"

"Well, she'd have to do that, wouldn't she?"

Bertie's words filled Josh with hope. Of course, Lavinia had to put on an act! That was her game! But he still couldn't quite believe what he'd seen. "She even asked for my photograph so that she can help them find me," he said.

"But she knows where you are, and so do they, so all that shows is that she's gained their trust without giving anything away."

Josh felt a sudden release of tension. He knew in his heart that Bertie was right. Lavinia was still the same girl that had walked into his house. Her life must be a nightmare compared to his. She had to be incredibly smart and brave to do what she did.

"Yes, it's a messy business, the role she's taken on," said Bertie, standing up, "And I can't blame you for having your doubts. But I'd be inclined to trust her." He patted Josh on the back and said, "I don't know about you but I'm hungry. Megs has been frying up some food. Let's go and have something to eat."

CHAPTER NINE

J osh thanked Megs for the meal. She'd done a good job and he could see from her smile that she felt pleased about it. He washed enough dishes to pass muster for helping with the washing-up, then hurried back on deck. He felt a painful urge to know what Machin was plotting next. He found a quiet spot on the other side of the deck beyond the hatchway and reached for his stone. This time it opened at once.

He stood beside her now on a stone balustrade he thought he recognised, looking down on the central square of the Last Resort. The huge, malodorous Saintly stood by her side. But her eyes were fixed on her stepdad waving to the cheering crowd in the square below.

Her stepdad smiled and rubbed his hands as he studied the crowd. He cast a questioning glance at Saintly and Josh felt sure he'd seen Saintly wink.

Most of the crowd were pirates. Why would they turn out to cheer the man who'd put their friends in prison? Some of them had even brought their children. Did they think they could buy their freedom by a show of devotion?

Lines of white vans had pulled up along the side streets. If anything happened now, the crowd had no means of escape. A tiny star of light made Lavinia blink. She turned her attention to the newspaper kiosk in the far right-hand corner of the square. The light flashed again, more distinctly this time, a glint of steel. She tugged at her stepdad's sleeve and whispered, "Dad! Dad! Someone's pointing a rifle at us."

"Shut up, Slug!" her stepdad warned through gritted teeth. With a fixed smile, he went on waving to the crowd.

A sound like the crack of a whip hit the stone lintel above her head. Her stepdad ducked and looked round, then patted his sides as if to make sure he was still alive. There were gasps from the crowd below, followed by screams and shouts and the sound of sirens. Pirates rushed in all directions, carrying or dragging their children towards the exits, while the police waded in from all sides, waving their batons and hauling and shoving people into those white vans. From megaphones rigged up at each corner of the square, a voice blared out, "This is an emergency! Keep calm, everyone, and go back to your homes. A curfew is in place. This is an emergency…" But they couldn't go back to their homes! All their exits were blocked. The Specials waved their truncheons and brought them down hard on the few stragglers still trying to leave. The white vans moved out of the side streets and circled the square.

The group on the balcony exchanged knowing glances. Machin brushed off the dust which had fallen from the lintel onto the shoulders of his blue suit. "When I said stage a shooting, Saintly," he said under his breath, "I didn't ask you to make it so realistic. That man nearly succeeded in killing me."

Saintly laughed. "Don't you worry, sir. That's Draco. If he was trying to kill you, he'd succeed." Machin glared.

"Too late for that now, isn't it, Daddy dear?" Lavinia said with a cheerful smile. "You'll have to get rid of him."

Saintly looked at her aghast.

"Otherwise, what would people think?" she asked in a reasonable voice. "He's an assassin, right? He tried to kill you."

"Right."

Her stepdad patted her on the shoulder and nodded. "Off with his head. You'll take care of that, Saintly?"

"Right."

Saintly fingered his neck. He'd come round to the idea. He looked as if he'd realised it wouldn't be his neck.

"What's a state of emergency?" she asked.

Her stepdad had already gone inside but Saintly placed a fatherly hand on her shoulder. He didn't seem to bear her a grudge. "Better follow him, eh? An emergency now, that's when the mopping up begins. People who threaten the state, they need to be got rid of."

"Why?"

"Because they threaten the state. If someone tries to shoot your leader, you can't hang around putting things to the vote; you have to take action."

"But you shot him yourself! Except you didn't – you only pretended to."

Saintly shrugged. "That's one way of looking at it."

"But it's the truth! Anyway, what kind of drastic action are you planning?"

Saintly tapped the side of his nose. "You'll see."

She smiled. "This Draco," she said slowly. "You're not really planning to kill him, are you?"

Saintly looked away. "I might be," he mumbled.

"Yea, you might be, but you won't."

He opened his mouth to deny it.

"I won't say anything," she said, "just so long as we stick together, right?"

Josh saw her smile as she followed Saintly into a small private office between the balcony and the assembly hall. He began to understand her game.

The office had a table big enough to seat six people, a sink and a drinks cabinet; no other furniture.

"*Proscriptions!*" *announced Machin, taking his place at the head of the table. He bared his teeth at Lavinia in a smile. "Not those little paper things you take to the chemist. That's spelt with an 'e'. Proscriptions"* – *he lingered over the word* – "*are when you eliminate all your potential enemies* – *or people whose death is likely to benefit you in any way. I have a list."* *He waved a piece of notepaper. "The pirate bankers. That's one thing pirates are good at; stealing our money. I'll come to them. Then there's the Flagsmiths. The parents of the boy. We'll keep them a little longer as hostages. Then there's the general."*

"*General Fairbones,*" *put in Saintly.* "*I told you, we should knock him out, sir."*

"*Yes, but we can't move against him, Saintly,*" *said Machin. "Not yet. He's too popular. We have to work on his image first; show the people that he is not the hero they imagined. We must tell them he's been secretly paid to work for us."*

"*Was he?"*

"*Oh Saintly, Saintly! Use your imagination. Politics is the art of the plausible."*

"*But that's not even plausible!*" *complained Lavinia. "Why would you want to pay people to fight against you?"*

"*Oh, I don't know, Slug! Who cares?"*

"*But you just said you had to show the people…"*

His fists banged the table. The knuckles had gone white. "I didn't say they had to believe me," *he spat out. "They just have to pretend to believe me. Or be re-educated. That's the bottom line. Can we get on?"*

"*Sorry, Daddy.*" *Lavinia stared at her lap.*

"*What's the matter, Slug? Thinking about mummikins?"*

Her shoulders had begun to shake. She took a deep breath and sat up straight, looking her stepdad hard in the eye. "No, should I be?" *she asked.*

Saintly laughed. "Some girl you've got there!"

Her stepdad didn't share the joke. "It depends whose side she's on," he mused. That mad gleam danced in his eyes.

"I'm on your side, of course. Otherwise, I wouldn't be here."

"Unless you were thinking of betraying me, Slug."

She stood up and stormed at him. "How dare you!" she shouted. "I've stood by your side all day, and yesterday too, and I warned you about the man with the rifle – only you knew it was a fake – but I tried to save your life and I would have done too and now all you can do is call me Slug, and talk about betraying you and–" She collapsed in tears.

Machin was smiling again. "Only joking, Slug," he said. "You'd better dry your eyes now. It's time for our meeting. And no more histrionics please. It worked once. It may not work a second time." He stood up to open the door. "Now, Lavinia, let me introduce you to our inner circle."

Three elderly men edged their way into the room, giving her a sideways glance as if to question her presence.

"My stepdaughter," Machin explained. He didn't bother to elaborate. He had his papers out in front of him and turned to the hunched figure who'd come in last and sat at the other end of the table. "Let's begin with our treasurer's report. Humphrey Mole? What have you got for us?"

Humphrey Mole was a small man with poor eyesight, squinting at rows and rows of figures that swam before his eyes. He looked up and immediately lost his place in the ledger, which prompted another furious fit of searching.

"We are at present in a state of flux," he announced in a dry, reedy voice, flicking through the pages. "There's a lot of money flowing out on essential capital expenditure – more weapons, more schools, more prisons, more government housing…"

"Yes, yes," said Machin. "But what about the money flowing in?"

Humphrey Mole beamed short-sightedly across the table. "In the short term," he said in his precise, mincing voice, "the flow *is just a trickle, but in the long term, thanks to our new ex-person law, I rather fancy that the trickle will become a flood."*

"Ex-person?"

"Under the new law, as soon you are sent to prison you become an ex-person. Therefore, anything that's yours belongs to us. The government, that is."

This report had put her stepdad in a good mood. He turned to Lavinia. "On the subject of economics, Slug, what's that paper stuff we all need to run our little island and keep everyone happy? I'll give you a clue. It comes in nice thick paper wedges and the new stuff has got my head on it."

The new arrivals laughed, three grinning skulls. Josh noticed that Saintly didn't join them. Lavinia had already gained an ally in this nest of thieves. He thought about what Machin had said about General Fairbones. He couldn't touch him yet because he was famous. His parents were famous too, and his stepdad was a colonist like Fairbones. They were keeping his parents as hostages. That meant they were safe for the moment but it wouldn't be for long.

Lavinia held her ground. "If you are referring to money," she remarked, "why not say so, Daddy? Are you going to raid the pirate bank?"

Machine raised an eyebrow. "I think someone's after your job, Saintly," he remarked. "I want you and your merry men to call at their houses and explain that the government – that's us – has decided to take over their bank. You know how it's done, Saintly. You will have to seize their computers to make sure they haven't shifted any funds before you arrest them. Then we'll have to put someone in to replace them. Mole, you've done time for embezzlement. You'd be ideal in that job; working for us, mind."

Saintly rubbed his hands. Mole blinked and hid his face in his papers.

"Do you want me to convert them into ex-persons, sir?" asked Saintly.

"No, Saintly, keep them alive for the moment. They may come in useful. Now, what's the news on the boy? Taken care of, is he?"

"Good news in a way," said Saintly, shifting in his seat and attempting a crafty smile. "Magnus Maxtrader will be landing here very soon on his annual visit. My spies tell me his yacht's moored in Paradise Harbour. And that's where the boy plans to visit him."

"So you didn't manage to eliminate him?" Machin allowed time for the nodding heads at the table to digest this titbit of news.

"No sir, but I'm convinced he'll be on that yacht."

"With Maxtrader."

Machin smiled, allowing the words to sink in.

"Yes sir. I thought all we have to do now is bomb the yacht."

"Did you? That's what you thought?" Machin paused. "Well, in future let's leave thoughts to the thinking department, which is clearly not yours."

Saintly sat with his head down, shoulders slumped, breathing heavily.

"No, that boy will be heading soon for Amaryllis," said Machin, "no doubt, on one of Maxtrader's helicopters."

"Yes, sir."

"So, if one of our friends were to follow him and track him down...no bombs, no guns; just a knife in the guts…do you think you could manage that, Saintly?"

"Yes, sir!"

Restored to favour, Saintly sat bolt upright at the table. He winked at Lavinia, as if to say, "You know me. I'll get it sorted."

Machin looked around the room and his eyes fell on Fleck. He had made his decision. He looked at Saintly and then he looked at Fleck. "No, Saintly," he said "This is a task which requires efficiency and speed – not really your strong points. I think I would prefer Dr Ronald Fleck to handle this one."

Saintly glanced at Machin and then glared across the table at Fleck. He made a move to leave the table, then thought better of it and sat down heavily, still smouldering.

Fleck watched this performance and gave a secretive smile. "I shall make the necessary arrangements," he said.

Josh felt a tremor of fear when he looked at the small man in the brown suit with round glasses and round blinking eyes. He noticed how his companions edged away from him. When Fleck stared at Lavinia, he smiled and licked his dry lips like a monitor lizard examining its next meal. He didn't fancy being Fleck's next meal either. No way! He'd make sure he and Megs never got caught on their own. But he'd have a weapon ready just in case!

Machin had turned to the wiry, irascible man on his immediate right. "We'll move on to defence. I think we are all aware that our ultimate success depends on the oblivion juice. What can you tell us about that, General Snort?

The general stood up to make his point, talking in quick jerky sentences with odd darting movements of his long, scrawny neck. "It's very delicate material, this oblivion stuff. I've brought some concentrated solution along with me just to show you what it can do." He pulled a cigar case out of his jacket pocket and fished out a corked test tube containing a small quantity of a dark red liquid. "If I were to open this test tube," he announced, in a cheery, decisive voice, "we would all be dead." Lavinia edged away from him as he opened it just a little to prove his point and gave it a quick sniff.

There was a nervous pause and Snort sat down. He rose again a little unsteadily and began again. "If I were to open this test tube...oh dear, I've forgotten what I was going to say."

"The man's an idiot," muttered Machin and then to Saintly. "Stuff it in a plastic bag and seal it quickly. The stuff's lethal. On second thoughts, stuff him in a bag too. He may be contaminated."

Everyone except Saintly backed away to the edge of the room. Restored to favour, he got up and walked round the table, grabbed the general by the shoulders and propelled him through the door. A single shot broke the ensuing silence, followed by a prolonged gurgle like a collapsing balloon. Saintly returned a few minutes later, wiping his hands. "He's an ex-person," he explained. "I stuffed the whole solution down his throat for good measure." He received a nod of approval from Machin which brought the old jauntiness back to his face.

Machin turned to his deputy and said, "Probably the best place for it, Dr Fleck, don't you think?"

"Undoubtedly," agreed Fleck, glancing up from his notes.

"Can you fill in the gaps in General Snort's account, Dr Fleck?"

Fleck's tongue darted around his lips, as he giggled and said in a dry, precise tone: "I suppose we should start with the juice. As this little episode has just shown, the concentrated material is deadly. As an experiment, we released the spray in cell 20 – just one small factory block. The liquid evaporated and the fumes filled the area in seconds."

"How many workers?" asked Machin.

"About thirty," said Fleck. "I am glad to be able to inform you that the spray not only wiped out the entire cell within seconds, but also wiped out three of the adjoining cells. The final body count was one hundred and two persons."

Josh saw that Lavinia had gone very still and clutched her neck. Luckily, Machin hadn't noticed.

"We're also working on a bomb," said Fleck. "By concentrating the liquid in a thin, metal casing, which fragments on contact, we can focus our weapon on a specific target."

"And how soon will this bomb be ready?" asked Machin.

"We hope to harvest the crop by the end of the week," Fleck said with a modest beam, folding his hand on the table and

sitting back. "Of course, we will need a large number of bombs to achieve our ultimate objective."

Machin had heard enough. "Well, gentlemen," he said, "I feel that it is appropriate to congratulate you all on your labours. We are, I feel, on the verge of an historic success. The general will shortly be at our mercy, the pirate bankers will be generously donating their money to our cause and pirates, throughout our little island, will soon be enjoying the fragrant smell of oblivion."

Lavinia followed her stepdad out of the room.

"You look half presentable, I suppose," Machin remarked as he parted company with his counsellors and strode down another red-carpeted corridor. "I have a crowd waiting in the grand assembly hall; ministers, generals, clergyman of the flat earth persuasion."

Lavinia jogged along behind him. "What about your inner council?" she asked.

"Best kept out of sight," he said, hurrying down the stairs. "This is supposed to be a democracy, remember, and the people forgot to elect that lot. Come on, we've got another floor to go."

As they reached the stage door of the assembly room, you could hear the expectant buzz of a large crowd. She followed her stepdad onto the platform where they sat, surrounded by grey-headed dignitaries.

Facing them in the grand hall under the gleaming chandeliers sat rows of important people in suits; generals, lawyers, business people, members of the criminal fraternity. She heard a murmuring and some sporadic handclaps, then shouts of encouragement from the Specials, standing at the back.

The reverend Billy Swagger of the Salvation Church stepped forward and mopped his brow. "Thank the Lord, I say, for a blessed escape!" he cried.

The Specials at the back of the hall shouted "Hear! Hear!"

The reverend Swagger continued: "Less than a year ago to this day, men without jobs walked the streets, begging for food, and the threat of violence kept us cowering in our homes at night. Unbelief was rife. Reggie Machin and his New Party put an end to all that!"

"Hear, hear!"

The reverend Swagger paused. "Of course, there will always be some that complain that we have lost some of our liberties," he said. "Just imagine how long it would take to make this little island safe for democracy if we had to do everything by the book. I ask you!

However, there is one book I believe in and I know Reggie Machin believes in it, too; The Book of Colonists. *That's why our church wants to increase its donation to Mr Machin and his New Party. And you know why we want to donate these additional funds? Because he has made this little island safe for colonists to live in!"*

He mopped his brow with a red cloth and reached in his pocket for a small book. "I'd like to conclude my welcoming remarks with a little passage from The Book of Colonists. *It's from the modernised version, of course, to make things nice and simple for good people like ourselves:*

'The Lord said. 'I've prepared a land in the far west of the world for you and your heirs to enjoy forever. So, you can grab it. It's yours. It's close to the world's edge, so guard it well, ensuring that none can fall off except unbelievers or other such riff-raff.'

Let's all fervently hope that this time will soon be upon us, thanks to Reginald Machin."

Josh noticed that not everyone clapped. A few brave souls even booed. The Specials stepped forward, pulled the offenders from their seats and frog-marched them out of the hall.

More speeches followed; speeches from generals praising the new army, speeches from businessmen applauding the economic boom, speeches from new politicians announcing improvements in transport, education and the prevention of crime. All thanks to Machin!

Machin rounded off the assembly with a brief and witty speech, thanking his audience for their support, humbly explaining that anything that his party had achieved was all thanks to them. Then he grabbed Lavinia's arm and hurried her off the stage.

Josh suddenly recognised that hall. It formed part of the old town hall which Machin must have taken over as his private palace. The hall itself was large enough to be used as a theatre. His mum had taken him there once, when he was small, to watch a Christmas pantomime. He remembered a magical evening when she sat there laughing at some of the jokes as much as he did. The memory brought tears to his eyes.

Chapter Ten

On the other side of the bay, they could see Maxtrader's huge three-masted yacht. Sailors in the trademark red and yellow livery raced to and fro on the deck.

"When are we going to speak to Maxtrader?" asked Josh.

Bertie leant against the hatchway, observing the scene through his binoculars. Just then he turned his attention to the jetty. His round face creased with anxiety. "That customs boat is heading towards us," he said. "If they reach us, we're in trouble. We'd better go now."

Josh ran to the helm and steered the dory in the direction of the yacht while Bertie hurried down to the cabin and returned in a grey pinstripe suit and a crimson tie. With his broad shoulders and confident stride, Josh scarcely recognised him. In one hand he carried an attaché case full of e-mails and the letter which Josh had given him from Lavinia. Josh noticed the customs boat slowing up as they approached the yacht.

They moored alongside the huge vessel and Bertie climbed on board. Josh saw him stride past a few sailors before one of them ran back and grabbed him by the shoulder, calling down to the cabin for assistance. More sailors gathered round but soon made way for two men in dinner jackets who emerged from the cabin with the smooth menace of disco bouncers.

"Bertie's in trouble," Josh whispered. "Should we join him?"

"He can handle this," said Megs. "Look! He's showing them the letter."

One of the bouncers waved an arm and the sailors slowly returned to their duties. Bertie said something and pointed to his case. The two bouncers didn't seem impressed. But they listened and then turned their backs on him and one of them picked up the phone.

Then things started to happen. One of them headed down the steps to the cabin, gesturing to Bertie to follow, while the other bouncer brought up the rear. Silence. Bertie looked at his watch.

"What's going on?" asked Megs.

Josh smiled. "Nothing too terrible," he said. "He's probably explaining about the letter and then the accounts. After that, we'll see."

After another ten minutes, they saw the two bouncers emerge from the cabin and stride across the deck. They disappeared over the gangway in the direction of the town. Several minutes later they returned, dragging a fat elderly man in a dinner jacket. They carried him, protesting, to the side of the yacht and tossed him over the side, leaving him to bob up and down and splutter and gurgle in the murky water until the owner of a nearby dinghy tossed him a lifeline.

"Who was that?" asked Megs.

"Who knows?" said Josh, rubbing his hands. "His accountant, perhaps. After this, they'll have to rename his firm 'Splutter and Gurgle.' Or it could be the editor of *The Daily Trumpeter*; one of Machin's cronies, at any rate. At least we know he's beginning to listen. Look out! Here comes another one!"

The two bouncers returned with another elderly man in a suit. This time, a photographer raced out after them. They waited until the camera was in position, then tossed their squealing victim so high in the air that he landed with a big enough splash to attract the attention of the whole harbour.

Finally, Bertie appeared on deck, chatting with the two bouncers and making them laugh. He came to the side of the boat and waved. "Welcome on board!" he shouted. "Maxtrader wants to see you!"

At first, it looked as if Magnus Maxtrader had forgotten them. They found him standing in the yacht's capacious dining room with a glass of brandy in one hand and a phone in the other. Waiters, agents and accountants lined the sides of the cabin, keeping very still, as this fat, bald man spluttered like a saucepan, throwing his boiling wrath in all directions. "Cancel the order!" he shouted down the phone. "Tell him to take the next plane out of the island…"

He reached for his other phone, which turned out to be the glass of brandy, and screamed, "Ed! Ed! Are you listening?"

It wasn't.

A small, hunched man in a pin-stripe suit appeared at his elbow and smoothly replaced the glass with a second phone. "Ed!" he shouted again. "You took your time. I want you to assemble all your staff, give them a week's wages and tell them they're sacked. Yes, all of them. No, that's all they're getting. Too damn right that's all they're getting! Yes, and then take the next plane out and report to me here."

He turned to the blue suit again. "Where's my glass? Someone took my glass. No, on second thoughts, get me *The Daily Trumpeter*. Who's their headline writer? Luke Sharp? Get me Luke Sharp."

He exchanged the phone for the brandy glass and sat down, frothing and drumming the table, while the man in the blue suit obtained the number. He grabbed the phone again. "Hey, Luke. That you, Luke? You got your headline ready for tomorrow? I want you to scrap it. I've got a much bigger story for you. This stuff is sensational. 'DISHING THE DIRT ON MACHIN.' Got a pen ready? Right. Take this down. 'Reginald Machin, self-appointed chief minister of Colony Island, has been making out that he's Mr Incorruptible, ridding the island of crime and so on, when in fact our fearless reporters have discovered that he's nothing more than a liar, a cheat and a thief.' What's that? Yes, Luke, it's a complete change of editorial policy. You may not like it, and if I had more time, I'd explain it to you. But I don't have time so all I'm asking you is to do is what I pay you for and effing well print it, and you can write the same stuff in the quality papers too, except make it twice as long and in posher language. Got that? Good."

He paused and wiped his forehead with a table napkin. "Where's my brandy? Just lay it on the table. Don't take my phone. I still need it. "You still there, Luke? Make sure this goes on the front page too. 'The Maxtrader yacht will arrive in the Last Resort in the early evening.' Yes, of course that's tomorrow but it won't be tomorrow by the time that newspaper comes out. Got that, Luke? Good."

Josh waited in the doorway with Megs who had just joined him. Maxtrader glanced in his direction. "You the boy with that stone thing? Come over here." He pointed to the other side of the large, square table.

Josh held his head up high and headed in that direction, with Megs at his side.

The bald, fat man glared at her and raised his arms in protest. "Who's that girl?" he snorted. "Get her out of here! I didn't ask that girl to join us."

Josh put an arm over Megs' shoulder. She fixed her black eyes on Maxtrader's face.

His red, sweaty cheeks wobbled with fury. "I said get her out of here!"

Megs wiped the froth from her cheek. Josh tightened his hold on her shoulders, but she wriggled away from his grasp.

A nervous hush fell on the cabin.

One of the bouncers stepped forward but Maxtrader put up an arm to stop him. "I'll deal with this," he shouted. "You go off and do what I pay you for."

He took a step towards Megs but she just stood there, looking small and skinny but with black eyes blazing defiance.

"You heard what I said! I want you out of here!" he shouted.

"Get stuffed!" said Megs.

Two more attendants lurched forward, ready to seize her. Josh stepped forward to protect her. Maxtrader went red in the face, eyeballs steaming.

Megs didn't change her position though Josh felt a tremble run through her.

Everyone in the room stared at Magnus Maxtrader. Suddenly he exploded in laughter. Tears rolled down his cheeks. He sat down and mopped his brow. "A girl of spirit!" he cried. "I like that girl!"

Dutiful titters from his attendants.

"What's your name?" he shouted.

Josh let go of her shoulder.

"My name's Megs."

"You got that everyone? Her name's Megs."

More laughter.

Megs hadn't finished. She took a step forward. "He came all the way here to bring you a letter from your granddaughter," she said, glancing at Josh. "It was his idea."

"Well, as ideas go, it was a good one. I've read the letter. That fat guy in the grey suit told me about it. My granddaughter, eh? Now she's a girl of spirit too. He nodded at Megs. "I can't decide which of you is worse. I'll do what she asks. You don't need to ask me again." He waved a dismissive hand to indicate that the audience was over.

Josh held Megs' arm again. He hadn't got to the important bit yet.

Maxtrader looked up. His mouth fell open. "You're still there!" he complained.

Josh leaned over the table. "I need to get to a helicopter," he said. "I have to go to Amaryllis and ask the council to come to our aid in Colony Island. I haven't got much time. I need to be there by tomorrow morning at the latest. Amaryllis is…."

"I know where it is," Maxtrader shouted. "You don't need to give me a geography lesson. What makes you think I'm going to find you a helicopter?"

Megs stared at him. "Because you have to," she said. "And I'm going with him. Because if it weren't for us, your own daughter could have died and you'd have gone on thinking Machin was good for business until you didn't have any business left."

"Because I have to," mused Maxtrader, rolling the idea round his tongue like a new taste. He started to laugh, nodding his head up and down till his eyes watered. "You want me to find you a helicopter *because I have to.* I like this girl! Is there anything else you want from me? No? Good. Better quit while you're ahead, eh? Wait there. I'll see what I can do for you!"

Bertie made his confident way across the room. "I would be enormously grateful if you could find room for me on your yacht. I have to join the rebel army, you see, and…"

Josh stared at him in surprise. He hadn't realised Bertie would be leaving them. But it made sense in a way. He wouldn't need Bertie's help in Amaryllis – not with Maxtrader organising the journey. And he'd be joining the Rebel Army in a day or two, himself. He'd explain that to Maxtrader later – when he'd calmed down a bit.

"You want me to sail several nautical miles out of my way just to drop you off at the other end of the island," Magnus Maxtrader shouted at Bertie. "Find a cabin for him," he shouted. "I suppose I owe him one for the information he's just given me." He turned to Bertie again. "Make yourself at home. I'm Father Christmas. Dinner will be in one hour. If you're late, you miss it. That's the deal. As for you two," he added. "Wait there! My assistant will sort you in a moment."

CHAPTER ELEVEN

The next morning, after a hearty breakfast on Maxtrader's yacht, Josh and Megs collected their belongings, said goodbye to Bertie and prepared to set out with fresh hope on the last leg of their journey.

Maxtrader himself thrust his thick arms over their shoulders, and led them out on deck, calling for a boat to take them to the quayside. They were good kids! They needed his help! So where was that boat? These kids needed to get to Amaryllis! He pointed to the black limousine parked across the water and shouted for Ed, one of the tall men that reminded Josh of disco bouncers, to stop leaning against a wall. The wall didn't need his support! It could stand on its own. That's what walls were for! So, if Ed wanted to keep his job, he could effing well come over and prepare to drive these kids to the heliport. He gave Megs' shoulders a squeeze, and thanked her for making him listen, when his mind was on other things, and he turned to Josh and gave him all sorts of advice about what to say and what not to say to the Pirate Council.

But where was that boat? There it was at last, heading towards them. He'd have words with that skipper! Then he remembered his daughter and shed a few tears of grief and anger when he thought of how that swine, Machin, had mistreated her and stolen his money. He thanked Megs again for reminding him, and said he wouldn't sleep another night until he'd rescued his daughter and his business from that awful man's hands.

Ed didn't look too pleased with his assignment. He grabbed their rucksacks in silence and led them down the steps to the dinghy. Then he shoved them into the back seat of the limousine parked on the quayside, switched on some loud music, and drove them through the drab suburbs of Paradise City towards Maxtrader's personal heliport a few miles out of town. He dropped them at a prefabricated whitewashed hut, at the edge of a small concrete runway, told them that the helicopter would depart on schedule, and all they had to do was go inside and wait.

Inside, the empty hall had everything you could wish for. They saw a long table at the far end, laden with cupboards full of snacks and a fridge full of free drinks. And, above it, stood a telescreen which you could operate from any of the remote-control devices placed on the round tables scattered round the hall. But Josh and Megs had eaten and seen more than enough that day, so they just dumped their rucksacks beside the nearest table and lay back in the comfort of two armchairs.

For a while, they just sat there and absorbed the silence. Josh closed his eyes and drifted into sleep. He awoke moments later to find Megs bending over him, whispering in his ear, "I just heard a toilet flushing." She pointed to the door on their right and added, "There's someone else in this building." As she spoke, a small man in a brown suit with round eyes and round glasses emerged from the toilet and approached their table. He smiled and sat opposite them. "My name's Ronald Fleck," he said, leaning over the table and offering them a damp hand to shake. "I often come here on business trips," he said, "This time I have come in a bit of a rush from Colony Island and I will be heading straight back there as soon as my business is concluded." He licked his dry lips and smiled at them, waiting for their response.

Megs just sat there and said 'hello' without any great show of interest, but Josh froze in his seat. He had to act fast, though it made him sick to think about it. His hand grasped the length of lead piping he'd picked up from the deck and stashed in his rucksack. Luckily, Megs had absorbed Fleck's attention. They were talking about cats. They both liked them, apparently, and Fleck had a cat called Mogs. It loved killing mice. Well, he wouldn't have a pet that didn't love killing something!

The piping was too heavy to hide so Josh stood up and pointed at the door at the end of the hall. "Look Megs!" he shouted, "it's Bertie!"

Fleck didn't turn his head. But Megs did. "Where? I can't see him!" she cried.

And that's when Fleck turned. Josh slipped behind Fleck's back in a flash and, in a blind act of madness, brought the lead piping down with a sickening thud on the side of Fleck's head.

Fleck groaned and toppled sideways from his chair, blood seeping from a cut above his ear.

"What have you done?" cried Megs, rising from her chair. "You could have killed him!"

"I wish I had!" he muttered "That's Ronald Fleck. He came over here to kill us! Quick! Pass me the rope from my rucksack."

Megs opened and closed her mouth in understanding and together they rolled Fleck over and tied his hands behind his back, emptying his pockets to discover a sharp-edged knife and a sealed test tube full of a familiar dark red liquid. Josh had half a mind to stuff the contents of the test tube down Fleck's throat.

At that point, a door at the far end of the hall opened and a man in a blue uniform announced that their flight was ready for boarding. When he saw the fallen body at their feet, the man cried, "What have you done?" and accused them of attempted murder but, when they explained that the body belonged to

Ronald Fleck, he took a more friendly view of things. He looked at the contents of Fleck's pockets and decided to call the police, agreeing to guard his body until they arrived. As for Josh and Megs, he advised them to leave at once, to avoid being delayed by the need to make a formal report.

Without further prompting, Megs pulled Josh towards the exit at the far end of the room. As he reached the door, Josh heard Fleck sit up and groan. "I'll be visiting your parents in prison," he whispered in a hoarse voice. "I shall enjoy that visit." With those words buzzing in his mind to disturb his dreams, Josh slammed the door of the departure lounge and followed Megs out to the runway where the helicopter stood waiting.

The noise of the helicopter made speaking impossible, so Josh and Megs sat in silence, gazing out of their separate windows and thinking their separate thoughts, as they passed over the vast stretch of sea surrounding the three large islands of Humphries, Windfree and Elephantia. But the memory of their near brush with death at the airport faded for a moment when they passed over a cluster of smaller islands in the southern seas. Then they started to chat again, and point excitedly at each new island unfolding below their eyes, always hoping that their special island would be the next.

They landed at last, in the early evening, in the warm, scented atmosphere of Amaryllis. As soon as they stepped out of the helicopter, a naval captain in a white uniform conducted them to his Land Rover and drove them on a three-hour journey, chatting all the way, through the forested interior of the island until they finally arrived at the mountain retreat of the Pirate Queen. Thanks to Maxtrader's extensive connections, the queen already knew about their visit and had hastily arranged a council meeting for the next day.

After a long night's sleep, his head buzzing with the sights and sounds of Amaryllis, Josh sat on a grassy slope beneath the shade of a jacaranda tree, looking down on the huge basin of the

Nirvana Stadium where the Pirate Council would hold its meeting. From this vantage point in the hilltops, he could see a scattering of dwellings dotted among the trees and then, in a compact mass, the little market town of Fortuna, with its ancient, whitewashed houses and narrow cobbled streets, toppling towards the sea. The pirates needed no excuse to break into song, often to the accompaniment of guitars, and even from this distance the sound of their singing was brought to him on the wind as a faint harmonious murmur.

After a peaceful night in Amaryllis, Josh had an uneasy feeling that the difficult part lay ahead of them. The queen was a large lady, dressed in long, flowing robes, with a loud voice and an imposing presence. She had informed Josh and Megs that the council would be held that evening. What would he say to them? They had so little time! The oblivion flower would be harvested by the time they docked in Colony Island. What if Ronald Fleck carried out his threat to visit his parents in prison and he wasn't there to help them?

Then he thought about Lavinia. What If she got found out? Then nobody would be safe. His thoughts kept directing him to that girl who lived in real danger every hour of her life. Even thinking about her made the stone grow warm in his hand.

He could see her now as her stepdad led the way down that red-carpeted corridor. He noticed how she hung back as far as she dared. She looked frozen with fear as she stooped by her bedroom door and watched him open that other door at the end of the corridor.

"Ah, Maria. I wanted to see you. Can you tell my wife that I won't be having dinner with her tonight? I'm busy."

"Your wife's not here, sir."

"What do you mean 'not here'?"

"Didn't you know that her father's yacht was due in the harbour this evening? It was in all the papers, sir."

"Yes, yes, I saw that, but she never mentioned she was joining it. I must stop her at once!"

"She's already gone, sir."

"What!!" His bloodcurdling scream echoed down the corridor.

"I am very sorry, sir. I thought she told you."

"Go away, Maria. I think I'm going to kill someone. For all I know it could be you."

Seconds later, Maria shot past her, bent on escaping his wrath, as fast as her short, stubby legs could propel her.

So Lavinia had achieved her mission; the first part of it at any rate. She'd promised to get his parents out of prison too. He'd seen enough to believe she had the bravery and cunning to see it through.

His shirt felt damp with sweat. He couldn't stay long in one position in this sultry heat without feeling the need to bathe in the freezing Pool of Miracles nearby. The waters of this pool issued from the snowy mountain top just visible as a bluish haze beyond the distant tree line. He could see the silvery thread of water cascading down the mountain into the blue mist of the Miracle Falls, a sheer drop of two hundred metres ending in the wide expanse of the Miracle Pool.

But a sharp pain between the eyes told him that Lavinia was in danger. He reached for his stone again. He stood beside her now. She had her back to the wall and her breath came in quick pants. She looked at her half-open bedroom door, as if she wanted to hide there, and then at that closed door at the end of the corridor. He could hear the muffled sound of Machin shouting and screaming and the crash of crockery being hurled against the wall. She stood there, waiting in stone-faced panic, for the door to open and the anger raging in that room to burst all over her. Then he saw Saintly approaching from the other end of the corridor at a swaggering stroll. The girl saw him too. You could see her shoulders relax and her eyes soften as she turned to face him.

"I heard someone kicking up a bit of a racket," Saintly said, *as he came up close to her. "Something the matter, girl?"*

"Sh!"

Saintly stopped and listened to the sound of crashing plates and furniture being hurled at the wall. The sight of Saintly had given her courage. She took a deep breath, like an actress who'd shaken off a bad attack of stage fright. "That's my stepdad," she *whispered. "Can I tell you something in confidence, Saintly?"* She stared up into his face him with her wide, innocent eyes.

Saintly rose to the bait like a hungry shark. "Something I don't already know?" he asked, coming even closer.

She lowered her voice and whispered, "I'm afraid he's gone mad."

Saintly shrugged. "A bit annoyed," he said, in a fatherly way. *"We all get annoyed sometimes."*

"More than that," she said. *"Don't you think he's losing the plot? I mean my mum held it all together, right?"*

"Right."

"And now she's gone. You know what that means?"

Saintly's brooding eyes absorbed the news. "Your mum's got some connection with Maxtrader, right?" he asked.

"She's his daughter."

"Hm. Bad news then. Not good for business, eh? Transport, stores, food supplies. All Maxtrader. Still, we should get through all right."

It had gone quiet in the room along the corridor. Lavinia must have noticed it too because she seemed confident enough to change the subject. "I'm worried about Mole," she said, twisting her hands and looking at the floor.

Saintly stroked his nose. "Humphrey Mole. Not up to it, you think?"

"He's a spy," she whispered. "Didn't you notice him in the meeting when we talked about the pirate bankers? He took notes."

"Get away! Not banknotes?"

"No, he had a notebook. I saw him. I even kept a page that he dropped on the floor. You know how short- sighted he is!"

"What did it say?"

"Just their names, and then a phone number, but you can guess the rest."

He grabbed her by the shoulders. "You done right to tell me, girl. We'd better act fast!"

"There's more. Can we keep this just between you and me?"

The door on his left opened. From the room beyond, a bloodcurdling yell echoed down the corridor. "Lavinia! Come here at once! Lavinia!"

Lavinia had to hide somewhere fast. Her bedroom was no escape. Machin would look for her there.

But there was a smaller door – the one Josh was leaning against. He tried the handle and found it locked. With all the force of desperation he willed it to open. To his relief and wonder, it swung free, revealing a dusty cupboard full of cardboard boxes and brooms. Lavinia turned and dashed inside.

Saintly did the rest. He reached the door in one stride and closed it, casually leaning his heavy frame against it.

Machin strode down the corridor and bore down on Saintly with haggard face and bloodshot eyes. "Where's my stepdaughter?" he demanded.

Saintly squinted up and down the corridor as if expecting her to appear at any moment. "I dunno, he said, rubbing his nose. "She was here a minute ago looking for her mum."

"What absolute nonsense! The scheming witch! She knew what her mother was up to."

"Is something wrong?" Saintly asked. "With your wife I mean?"

"She's gone." The anger in Machin's voice had gone flat.

"I'm sorry about that. We didn't know."

"What do you mean, 'we'?" A quick stab of fury.

"Me and Lavinia. She was more worried about you."

A snort of disbelief. *"Oh Saintly, Saintly! If you believed that, you'd believe anything!"*

"On account of Mole."

Machin didn't seem to hear. *"When I think how I trusted that girl,"* he ranted, *"how I fell for her cunning suggestions, how I–"* he stopped in his tracks. *"What did you say about Mole?"*

"He's a spy. You know them bankers? He was going to phone them – warn them about our plans. We found their telephone number in his notes."

"We?"

"Well, Lavinia really. She did what you asked her to do, kept a check on your friends. She was that concerned for you."

Machin stood open-mouthed. Then he gave an astonished laugh. *"Lavinia did all that?"* he asked. *"Good old Slug! Well, no time to waste! You'd better grab those pirates before they escape. I'm off to find Fleck. We have to sort out the Mole."*

He strode off down the long, red-carpeted corridor. As the sound of his footsteps faded away, the cupboard door burst open and Lavinia nearly fell into Saintly's arms.

"Thanks, Saintly. You saved my life."

"Yea? Well you can save mine one day."

"Thanks, Saintly."

She opened her eyes wide in gratitude. *"I was thinking, Saintly,"* she said, twisting her hands again in a pose of bashful innocence.

"Yes, my girl."

"We have to help each other, right?"

"Right." He didn't seem too sure about it.

"I mean like you saved me from my stepdad just then."

"He got a bit excited. That's all."

"Yes, well, when he gets excited, people tend to wind up dead. Like Mole, for example. I say something, you say something and we end up like Mole."

Saintly grabbed her shoulders again. "You ain't thinking of telling him nothing about me?"

"That's my point, Saintly. You saved my life just then. I want to help you, the same way you helped me. That way we both stay alive and benefit."

Saintly dark eyes brooded on this statement. "Who did you say benefits?" he asked.

"We both do."

"Right."

"Well, you mainly."

"Fair enough then."

"Those pirates," she began. "They've got a lot of money, right? It would be a pity if it all went to waste."

He looked at his watch. "Don't you worry, my girl. I'll get there on time. I'm sure of it. We'll lay our hands on their funds."

She hesitated. "Yes, but when you've got the money and it's all been handed over to my stepdad and it's been spent on weapons and prisons and all that stuff…" She didn't complete the thought.

"It's a lot of money," he mused.

She giggled. "I know it's a bit naughty, but I was thinking…" Again, she hesitated. A crafty expression flickered in his eyes. "Go on, girl, I'd love to know what you was thinking."

She faced him squarely, twisting her hands again. "I was thinking, how about if you didn't arrest them but helped them escape instead? They would pay you a whole load of money for your help and you could go back and tell my stepdad that you were too late. Mole had already tipped them off."

A slow smile crept over Saintly's face and he nodded. "I like it girl, I like it," he said.

Lavinia grinned. "So do we have a deal?"

"It's a deal. A pity about Mole," he added with a knowing wink. *"Mind you, I never did see that note you found in his papers."*

Josh slowly surfaced from his vision. He rubbed his eyes and replaced his stone in his pocket. Then he started to laugh. That girl had not only saved her mother and the pirate bankers but she'd got rid of Mole and she held Saintly's life in the palm of her hands; and all that from the verge of disaster. She was playing a dangerous game and deserved all the help she could get. Maybe he had helped her this time. He could have sworn that door was locked when he leant against. Had it opened of its own accord or had he willed it to open?

He saw Megs approaching up the slope. Her black hair looked soft and silky and she wore sandals and a loose-fitting garment of dark red silk, pinned with gold braid at the shoulders and waist. She looked good in that outfit, but he felt shy about telling her. "Where have you been?" he asked, gazing up at her.

Megs gave a secretive smile. "The queen asked to see me again," she said.

"What did she want?"

"Nothing special. She gave me this." Megs pointed to her dress. "What do you think?"

"What am I supposed to think? It's a sheet."

He expected her to be annoyed but she just grinned. "Who cares?" she said. "Feel it. It's so light and soft. It's brilliant in this heat. Besides, I need it for the ceremony. You'll need to smarten up too,"

"The council's not till later!" he protested.

"Yea, but you can't speak before the council until you've come of age. That's the law. So you have to speak to the queen beforehand. How old are you, anyway? You never tell me anything."

"Thirteen! My birthday's today! I forgot all about it!"

"I know."

"Then why did you say -?"

"The queen told me," she said triumphantly. "You were born here, remember? They do have birth certificates, you know. Anyway, I bought you this." She blushed and shoved a small package into his hands.

He got to his feet, not sure what to say. He didn't usually get presents, except from his mum. His stepdad taught him how to do stuff, like climb mountains or catch fish. He liked that sort of present too.

"Thanks, Megs," he said. "I wasn't expecting this. What is it?"

"Open it and see."

Josh unwrapped the present to discover a small, ornately carved rosewood box. Inside, he found a silver chain and, hanging from the chain, a little velvet pouch.

"Thanks, Megs, it's beautiful," he said, examining the object in awkward curiosity. "What's it for?"

"You know that stone thing you always carry in your pocket? You might lose it! I thought you could wear this chain under your shirt where nobody can see it, with the stone safely stashed in the pouch." She shrugged and added "Well, it was only an idea."

"Thanks, Megs, it was a good idea."

"Then do it!"

"Okay."

Under Meg's searching gaze, Josh placed the stone in his pouch and put the silver chain round his neck. It felt good. "What next?" he asked.

Megs blushed. "Now you're supposed to kiss me," she said.

He leant forward and kissed her lightly on the lips.

"Happy Birthday," said Megs, blushing. "The stone's covered by your tee-shirt," she said in a more normal, matter of fact voice. "It's safer that way. Now you have to meet the queen and collect your certificate."

"But I have to wash and get changed!"

"Well, hurry! The council starts in an hour."

CHAPTER TWELVE

J osh stooped through the circular door of his box-shaped bedroom, high in the swaying branches of the jacaranda tree. As he washed and put on clean clothes, he thought about what he would say to the council. But the more Josh thought about his speech, the more he felt sucked into that other world so many miles away. Something horrible had just happened there; something that sent a shudder right through him. He sat on his bed and reached for his stone.

He followed Lavinia with his thoughts into the small private room behind the balcony. Saintly tapped her on the shoulder and whispered 'job done' as he followed her into the room. Machin stood up to greet them with his crocodile smile stretching from ear to ear. He cast a sidelong glance at Ronald Fleck who wore a white bandage stretched slantwise across his head. His face had a yellowish tinge, making his smile more sickly than usual.

"First things first," said Machin, *"I am sure we would all wish to commiserate with our dear Dr Fleck. I send him on a simple errand, to prevent the boy from reaching Amaryllis, and what happens? The boy – a simple schoolboy of 12 or 13 – bashes him on the head with a length of lead piping and he is forced to come home under police escort."*

"Better luck next time, Fleck," said Saintly, grinning from ear to ear. Lavinia at this point had a severe coughing fit, which left her reaction to be guessed at.

"However, let's move on to the point of this meeting," said Machin, holding up a small statue the size of a chess piece. "I want to show you this delightful figurine. Does he remind you of anyone? He set the figure on the table for them all to see.

"My God," said Saintly, "It's an exact replica of General Snort."

"Nearly right, Saintly; keep going."

"It's not my mother; that's for sure. She had a bit more flesh on her. I could have sworn it was a replica of Snort; down to the last dribble, I'd say."

"Yes. It was his last dribble, I suppose," said Machin, his eyes darting round the room like a python in search of more to whet his appetite. His eyes rested on Mole. "You see, it's not a replica. Tell him, Dr Fleck."

All eyes bent forward, drawn by morbid fascination, towards the human chess piece on the table.

"Well," said Fleck, glad of the chance to restore his credibility, "our scientists have found a way of harnessing the oblivion juice. Mixed with molten amber, it not only kills you but has the power to contract your cells; in other words, to shrivel you to the size of a nut."

"So this," said Machin, tossing his chess piece in the air and catching it, "is the real General Snort. I think I shall varnish him and put him on my mantelpiece."

Saintly and Mole edged towards the other end of the table.

"Well, on to other things," said Machin, putting the figure back in his pocket. "You may have noticed that the plans we made at our last conference didn't quite work out the way we intended." Machin paused and brushed a speck of dirt off his sleeve. He studied the four faces at the table. "The pirate bankers; it has just come to my ears that they have closed their *bank, shifted all their funds to a tax haven and disappeared to Crown Colony. And, as I just mentioned, the boy has succeeded in reaching Amaryllis. My colleague, Fleck, assures me that someone must have tipped him off. But nobody outside this room knew about our plans. No, gentlemen, I have to say that there is a mole in our midst."*

Silence hung in the air. Saintly seemed absorbed in watching the progress of a fly across the ceiling. Fleck's face had emerged from his papers. He leaned back and licked his dry lips as he watched poor Humphrey Mole holding the sides of his chair, in an effort to stop himself from shaking.

Machin's face stopped twitching and relaxed into a smile. "Never mind!" he said. "I'm a forgiving man and who's to say I was not mistaken? Let's not dwell on the past but the future and the success it will bring. Let's drink to our continuing success. One moment please."

Reginald Machin reached into his drinks cabinet where a tray had already been prepared.

The idea of Machin as a forgiving man hadn't caught on. Lavinia stared at the table. Nobody cheered. The clock on the wall ticked on.

Saintly fished something from the inside pocket of his leather jacket, a sudden movement which caused everyone at the table to duck. He looked around him in surprise, holding up his small colonist bible. "You remember I don't drink alcohol," he explained, "It's against my religion."

"Nor do I, I'm afraid," said Fleck, in watchful anticipation.

Josh looked at Mole, whose face had gone white. Machin seemed not to have noticed. He held each glass up to the light before laying them on the table in front of him. "Indeed, gentlemen," he said, "I remember your various…hm… preferences. Let me see, these glasses are for you…Saintly, Fleck. And Lavinia, I suppose you're included. Blackcurrant juice is all I could muster, I'm afraid, while Mole and I will share the delights of pink champagne. To your health, everyone."

They all looked at Humphrey Mole. His hand shook so badly that he could hardly get the glass to his lips. Feeling the force of their eyes upon him, he tipped the liquid towards his mouth. The first sip had an instantly calming effect. He went rigid and Machin leaned over and tipped the rest down his throat.

Josh watched in awe as Mole stiffened and deflated. One moment, his head was about a foot above the table and the next it had sunk a few inches. Very soon, only the pink dome and a few grey whiskers remained visible.

"From Mole to a manikin, fit for my mantelpiece!" cried Machin. "Let's leave poor Mole to discover his true size and press on with our plans. Come on, everyone, concentrate! We've had our little bit of fun. Now we have work to do." He turned to Fleck. "How is our spray progressing?"

Fleck's eyes were riveted to the sight of Mole's head disappearing below the level of the table. He licked his lips and referred to his notes. "I'm not sure if you've heard of Patience Grove? It's a housing estate on the east side of town."

"I've heard of it! Get to the point."

"I suppose you could say we've run out of Patience."

"What do you mean?"

"They're all dead." Fleck licked his lips and referred to his notes again. "You see, my idea was to try out the concentrated solution on a small pirate community of two or three hundred families. We sprayed the estate from the air first, and then added the solution to their water supply. Of course, we found five or six colonist families living on the estate, but we took the precaution of removing them beforehand."

Machin gave a thoughtful nod. "All in all, a very creditable effort, Fleck," he said. He looked at Saintly and Lavinia for their approval.

"Wow," said Lavinia, putting her head down and nearly choking on her blackcurrant juice.

"Yes, well. A drop in the ocean," said Machin. He turned to Fleck again. "Talking of drops, when will you be ready to drop our bombs on the rebel camp?"

"Very soon. We have run out of the concentrated solution for the time being, but the plant will be harvested in the next few days, and then we should have more than enough to wipe out a whole island."

"Or half of it?"

"Yes, of course, half," Fleck agreed, staring down at the table, as if suddenly forced to halve his ambitions.

Machin turned to Saintly. "Now, Saintly," he said, "Just in case our bomb doesn't do the trick, "how many divisions can we send to help our friend, Dr Fleck, wipe out resistance on the west coast? Six? Seven? I should think seven should be enough, with the aid of helicopters and machine guns. After that, perhaps, we can turn our attention to the Federation. I'm already receiving letters of support from staunch colonist elements on our sister islands. Discovery Island is an easy target. Crown Colony is the glittering prize."

He paused and drummed his long fingers on the table. "Discovery Island has just shot down one of our helicopters," he said, looking at the nodding heads and letting his eyes rest for a moment on the fast- disappearing head of Humphrey Mole. "So that's a starting point. As soon as you've gathered in the harvest, let's reveal our weapon to Discovery Island. I mean, just show it to them, explain its potential. We don't want them thinking they can threaten us."

Fleck raised one of his soft hands. "I would be happy to undertake that duty."

Her stepdad paused. "No, I was thinking of sending Draco."

Saintly stared hard at the table.

"Draco's dead," Lavinia put in quickly. "Don't you remember your orders?"

Machin didn't seem to be listening. He was peering down at the shrinking remains of Humphrey Mole. "Sorry, Slug, you were saying something about orders? Draco should be dead – that's true – but he was very much alive when I spoke to him this afternoon. Still on your to-do list, Saintly?"

Saintly wrung his hands. "Sorry, sir. I've just been waiting for the right moment."

"A pity. I had been hoping to add him to my collection. I do hope you won't keep me waiting too long, Saintly. Otherwise, I might be forced to look for a substitute."

Saintly sat with his massive shoulders hunched at the table. Machin didn't seem to notice. He stood up to dismiss them. Take a last look at our dear Mr Mole," he suggested. "In a little while, he will be reduced to the size of a walnut. Well, everyone, that's all for now. Unless I can tempt anyone to another drink?"

Josh heard Machin's manic laughter as they all shot out of the room. The noise merged with the sound of someone calling his name.

"Josh! Did you hear me? I've been waiting nearly half an hour."

"Sorry, I've just had a dream," he said, looking up from the bed and blinking as he remembered where he was.

"We need to make a move," said Megs, standing in the doorway.

"More than a dream; a vision."

"Well, make your mind up. Which was it?"

"Listen, Megs. This is serious. You know Patience Grove?"

"Of course I know Patience Grove! I used to live there. What of it?"

So Josh told her, and Megs cried, but she didn't cry as much as he expected because she was only four years old when her parents died and she moved from Patience and came to live at the Hilltop Farm. But she started to cry again when she thought of all those people and how they'd died. And then she thought of Bertie going off to fight for the Rebel Army and how Machin planned to bomb them from the air and kill them too. And she wanted to know about Josh's visions and whether they were true, and he had to explain everything from the very beginning.

He followed her out of the room, his mind still stuck in Colony Island and the words of Ronald Fleck.

Megs grabbed his hand and pulled him along. "Your parents will be safe. I know it!" she said.

"Thanks, Megs," he said.

"Lavinia will keep her promise," she said. "You have to trust her."

By this time, they had caught up with the crowd of pirate families hurrying along the woodland path to the Nirvana Stadium.

"They are all in a hurry to get the best seats," Megs whispered. "We don't have to worry as we'll be on one of the speakers' tables."

"How do you know?"

"The queen told me. Have you got your speech ready?"

"I don't know. I'll think of something."

Meg's question hit a nerve. Still, speaking in public couldn't be worse than climbing down a well or facing Ronald Fleck. His island was in danger. It needed their help. What more could he say? "I think I'll make it short," he said.

"Good luck! These pirates don't do short."

"Thanks, Megs."

"Oh, look!"

She pointed to the view on their right, where the hills formed a natural arena, the slope on the far side being covered by rows of wooden benches. It was in this direction that the crowd now headed, spreading out like geese to cover the widening path and find seats as near as possible to the front row.

"Keep walking," said Megs. "Our seats are on the other side."

A few yards further on, a young lady in a long scarlet robe, with the words 'Amaryllis Council' emblazoned on a silver sash, tapped Josh on the shoulder. "The queen is expecting you both," she said. "She is waiting in the tent with the sages and notables. It's not far."

A hundred yards further on, they came to another gap in the trees and gazed down at a long line of trestle tables covered by white cloths. "Those are the speakers' tables," said the official, leading them down the steps. "We have to walk past them to get to the tent." As they hurried across the open space in front of the tables, Josh saw that the audience would be closer than he imagined. The front seats were almost in touching distance. Some of the crowd were already seated, some scrambling for a place on the benches. Their mingled voices thundered in his ears. Some even stood up and pointed in his direction. His stomach churned at the thought of making his speech.

The 'tent' at the edge of the arena turned out to be more like a marquee, crowded with elderly sages in white cloaks. Only the Pirate Queen wore a cloak of royal purple. She barged her way through the throng and approached them with open arms at the entrance to the marquee. Queen Bellagrossa was not only large but had a deep voice and a commanding presence. She gave them the royal hug which left them squashed and breathless. Like many pirates in this part of the world, she came originally from the southeastern island of Portarabia and spoke with an unfamiliar accent that mixed its b's and p's, and confused 'next' with `nickers.' She also liked to season her conversation with random words like 'sometime' and 'maybe', which Josh found quite confusing.

"Ah Meg!" she cried. "Bery nice girl. Bery, bery nice to meet you, sometime…yes! For me, I think like princess. Like my daughter. Truly, I think it! Come and sit nickers to me." She grabbed Megs' hand and pulled her through the crowd of notables to a seat beside her throne. "Is pleasure for meet you one more time in the face. When I see you, I think oh so beautiful! Maybe...Yes."

"Thank you," said Megs, looking around as if not quite sure where to hang the compliment.

"Today," continued the queen, "I promise it, is the most boring day of your life. Maybe. Also for you Josh. Come closer. Let me look at you. You are to me, how to say it, like my son. Is true." She squeezed Josh's cheeks in a sign of affection that made him wince. "Important but also young. And I hear you will make one speech. Is good, no? Today, everyone make speeches." She sighed and a huge shudder ran down her body.

"Do you think the council will agree to help us?" asked Josh.

"Of course, why not? We live in a demogracy," she said. "I tell them what to think and they think it." She clapped her hands. "Is enough!" she said. "The people are arriving. You go now. Is enough." She shooed them out of her tent and prepared her long-suffering face to meet the challenge of the evening.

The official reappeared to escort Josh and Megs to the far end of the trestle tables. The other sages and notables gradually wandered out of the marquee and took their places.

Then two pirate girls came forward to face the crowd and blew a long blast on their horns and Queen Bellagrossa, amid cheers, took her seat on her throne. Just as she had got installed, Josh saw a man he recognised, hurrying to find a place at the other end of the table. "John Bosworthy," he whispered to Megs. "That's John Bosworthy, my stepdad's lab assistant," as he watched his hasty struggle to get into his white robe. John Bosworthy's presence gave him a ray of hope. He'd be able to confirm what was going on in Colony Island. And he'd know about his parents. He took a fond look at him. He was a shy but friendly fellow who didn't look more than eighteen, but his stepdad had said he was at least twenty-five and a very clever scientist.

The crowd cheered as they observed the sacred albatross, soaring over the trees and making a spectacular, juddering, landing on the stage. The arrival of the albatross meant that the conference had begun.

The queen stood up and introduced the sages and notables, explaining – to roars of approval – that the conference would be devoted to their beloved brethren on Colony Island.

Then came the speeches. Josh sat with Megs at the opposite end of the table from John Bosworthy. Knowing he had to speak last made him tense and fidgety, but as the afternoon wore on, he couldn't help dozing off – though he woke up and cheered with the crowd when the Sage of Military Science explained that they wouldn't be sailing in a fleet of antiquated corsairs but a single, fully equipped modern battleship.

Two hours had passed when it came to John Bosworthy's turn. And knowing he'd be next made Josh sit up and listen with added interest. John Bosworthy patted his short, fair hair, blinked and looked around him. When he began to speak, Josh noticed that, without raising his voice, he spoke so clearly that everyone could hear him. And he sounded quite natural, as if he were at home speaking across the dinner table.

"I hope you will excuse me for arriving late for this very important council," he began, "but I only managed to escape from Colony Island this morning. I expect you will all want me to tell you how things are on that island today, but first I'd like to tell you how all our troubles began.

"I grew up on the Island, of course, and until two years ago pirates and colonists rubbed along pretty well – as they have done for centuries throughout the western isles. Then the crops failed and people lost their jobs, and that's when everything went pear-shaped. Our local newspaper, *The Daily Trumpeter*, fanned the flames by telling us that it was all the fault of the pirates. Gangs of unemployed colonists – and pirates too, of course – gathered in 'The Last Resort' and traded insults. And then a politician called Machin came along. He'd made a name for himself in show business, of course, so he knew how to win over the masses, and he promised that his 'New Party' would solve all our problems.

"Well, he didn't solve them, of course. He simple rounded up thousands of pirates and threw them in prisons or labour camps. And now he is bent on genocide. So that's it. Without your help we are done for!"

This speech was greeted with cries of outrage and fury, shortly followed by cheers when the queen arose from her seat to announce that the final speaker would be the young Guardian. Josh heard repeated cries of 'Our Guardian, let's hear him!' and then a few voices, shouting 'Then shut up and let him speak!'

As he rose to his feet, Josh no longer felt nervous because John Bosworthy had given him something more to say. 'This war is not against colonists," he began. "My best friend is a colonist, and his dad is fighting in the rebel army beyond the mist. General Fairbones is a colonist and he is leading that army. John Bosworthy is a colonist and he has risked his life coming here tonight. My stepdad is a colonist and he's over there, sitting in prison. Machin is the enemy and a small group of evil men, armed with nothing more than a little red flower, the flower of oblivion. In a few days, that flower will be harvested and the juice extracted and used to make a deadly weapon. When he gets that weapon, Machin's not going to stop at Colony Island. He has already threatened Discovery Island. Crown Colony will be next and so on, until he has made himself lord of the western isles. So, what do we need? We need that battleship and we need it now. And we need soldiers to join our small rebel army beyond the mist. We need them now. Can you help us?"

"Was that long enough?" he whispered to Megs, as he sat down.

Megs gave him a hug. "It was brilliant," she said. "I didn't think you had it in you."

To his surprise, Josh looked up to see a forest of hands volunteering to man the fleet or join the rebel army. Queen Bellagrossa stood up and waited patiently for the noise to subside before she announced. "People of Amaryllis, I see you all have decide what is to do. The sheep, it will leave tomorrow at the rise of the sun. I want you all go home and, if you want be on that sheep, please to stop at this table and tell your name to one of our official persons."

Josh and Megs stood and watched a steady stream of pirates, men and women, hurrying towards the trestle tables to book their places on the battleship.

Chapter Thirteen

J osh tossed and turned on his bunk, feeling the unending rise and fall of the ship through the gentle waves. He had no idea how long the battleship had been at sea. He kept trying to count the days on his fingers, but the answer kept coming back – too long; too long sitting idle while his parents lay in gaol and Lavinia stood in terrible danger. Why hadn't he thought of that before? He felt another fit coming on and his arms flailed around, searching for his stone until he remembered the silver chain round his neck and the pouch where it was safely stowed.

He could see Lavinia quite clearly now. She stood on a balcony. And the man beside her was Saintly. He sensed her fear.

"Is it safe to talk?" she asked.

Saintly didn't answer. He had his back to her, staring out at the empty square. "He knew about Draco," he muttered.

"Listen, you don't think it was me that told him?"

"I dunno."

"I didn't go near him since we last talked. I had no opportunity to tell him."

"Maybe."

"Besides…" She put on her girlish voice. *"I thought we had a pact,"* she said, *"like we agreed to help each other."*

"Oh yea."

"He's mad, you know."

"So, you say."

"Oh, come on, Saintly! He's a stark raving nutter. We have to look at our options."

"Like?"

"Like what happens when he's gone. We don't want to be dragged down with him. At least you don't. I'll probably be all right. I'm just a girl."

He still had his back to her.

"Come on, Saintly! I'm trying to help you."

"Spit it out, then."

"I'm thinking of the boy's parents, the Flagsmiths. It would be useful to have them on our side. We need to make contact with them now so we have friends we can turn to when all this is over."

Saintly rounded on her like a mad bull, eyes blazing. "Are you crazy, girl? The Flagsmiths? You're like one of them! Keep away from me! Your stepdad needs to know about this!"

She held up two hands and looked him straight in the face. "Come on, Saintly! I mean, is that wise? To have it all come out? How you as good as told me that you disobeyed orders over Draco and how you warned off the pirate bankers and how you accepted a packet of money from them? My stepdad will go mad!"

"That was you!" he spluttered. "That was all your doing!"

"Better explain that to him yourself, Saintly, because it certainly doesn't look that way. Not when he sees the money! I certainly didn't accept any money from those bankers."

Saintly turned his back on her again. When he spoke, his voice choked with bitterness. "You set me up, girl! You had this planned all along."

"I'm not clever enough for that, Saintly. I'm just trying to help, like you helped me. In case things don't work out with my *stepdad, we've got friends, right? Surely that's better than being an ornament on a mantelpiece?"*

"What are you asking me to do?" he asked in a flat voice.

"Release the boy's parents from gaol. Stage an escape. Whatever. Tell them they are free to go home. I'm sure they will be very grateful."

"You're sure of a lot of things," he said, with a scowl that suggested he'd just swallowed a maggot.

Josh leapt out of his bunk, put away his stone and pumped the air with his fists, expressing his joy in a single cry of, "She's done it!"

"Who's done what?" asked Megs, who'd come to wake him up. "Talking to yourself?"

"I dunno," he said. "I've just had a vision. That girl I told you about. She's getting my parents released?"

"Are you sure? Can she do that?"

"Yes, sure!" He suddenly felt he heard a familiar voice talking outside the cabin. "What's the time?" he asked, observing the light through the porthole. "Where are we?"

"It's mid-morning – I just came to tell you that we've arrived!"

"Arrived...where?"

"Colony Island, of course! The other side of the mist. Bertie's here waiting for you, and Sandy will be here shortly."

"I'd better get dressed then. I'll join you in a bit."

Josh emerged from his cabin to find Bertie's familiar face smiling in his direction as he chatted with Megs and a member of the crew. He looked strangely out of place in a peaked cap and army fatigues.

Bertie pointed towards the misty shore. "That's where we are heading," he said. "The ship's not stopping here. It's heading along the coast to train its guns on 'The Last Resort' and block the immediate threat to Discovery Island. You and Megs are coming with me to meet the rebel army camped beyond the mist.

Josh saw a motor launch shooting towards them out of the mist. Megs gave a scream of delight and started to jump up and down and wave at the boat. "That's Sandy. Look, Josh! Look! And that's his dad at the wheel."

Josh felt another surge of renewed hope. He hadn't expected staunch colonists like Sandy's dad to go as far as joining the rebel army.

"Are you coming?" Megs called, in a hurry to descend the ladder onto the launch.

Sandy's dad helped them aboard. Sandy waited as Josh and Megs piled in on either side of him. He smiled in an embarrassed sort of way. "We were sent to collect you," he said.

"Lucky you explained that," said Josh, throwing an arm over his shoulders. "I mean I thought you might be going fishing."

"In a motor boat?" asked Sandy. "If I was going fishing–"

Megs gave him a nudge. "Shut up, Sandy! He's teasing you. Where are we heading now?"

Sandy's dad sat at the tiller beside Bertie. He had to shout to make himself heard above the spray and the roar of the motor. "Further west along the coast. Hold tight, you three. It's a bit choppy but it won't be long now."

After a while, the noise dropped as the boat came close to the shore and edged its way westward, past the mist.

Sandy's dad was a large, mild-mannered man with fair hair and freckles like his son. "We're heading for the caves," he explained. "There's a whole network of caves on the southwestern tip of the island. Some of them stretch for miles."

"Will we be doing any fighting?" asked Josh.

Sandy's dad considered the question in his slow way. "There's not many of us and the more we fight the more we run the risk of giving our position away. At the moment, they seem to think we come and go through the mist."

"But if we are not going to fight, what–?"

"What are we here for? Is that your point?"

"I suppose so."

"Spying, mostly. On the opposite headland, Machin is developing his oblivion bomb. We need to know how the work is progressing, obstruct it where possible and just hang in there until we can gather more recruits."

"Is that easy?"

"No." Sandy's dad concentrated on steering.

They had passed the mist now and Josh could see their probable destination; a little sandy cove tucked away in a fold of the cliffs. "I'd better warn you, Josh," said Sandy's dad, as they headed for the cove, "that you must be prepared for quite a reception when you get to the top of the cliffs."

"Will we be under fire?"

Sandy's dad laughed. "No, nothing like that. But you're the boy with the stone, remember? Apart from a few colonist oddities like myself, the rebel army are loyal pirates to a man and you're their Guardian now. You're a celebrity. They're expecting great things of you."

"Oh." Josh looked at Megs. Fortunately, she hadn't stopped talking to Sandy since she got on the boat so she hadn't heard that bit. "What shall I say?" he asked.

"Just act the part, even if you don't feel it. Pirates like a bit of bravado. You're a confident chap, Josh. You'll manage it."

Josh grinned.

As they beached the boat, Sandy's dad pointed to some steps cut in the rock. After a short climb, they reached a narrow strip of land bordered by rocks on either side. Where the rocks ended, the land opened out into a flat, grassy plain, stretching as far as the eye could see. The rebel army were trying to protect the narrow strip with an earth wall. Pirates in red scarves knotted at the back worked the length of the wall, digging and carrying earth in wheelbarrows and buckets. Several heads turned when the new arrivals reached the top of the steps.

An excited mob clustered round Josh, inspecting him and touching his clothes. "Are you the boy with the stone?" cried one. "He seems quite young, don't he? May we see it – the stone, I mean?"

He held it out for them to see and touch.

"Don't let this go to your head," whispered Megs at his side.

"I won't."

"Well, don't."

Three old men, with faces tanned and scarred by wind and toil, edged their way to the front. "You're the new Guardian, right?" asked one of them, with head bent to one side, peering into Josh's face. "You've come to help us, right?"

"Give the lad a chance, Ernesto!" his friend protested. "He's just arrived!"

Ernesto rounded on his friend. "I know he's just arrived. I can see he's just arrived. Come off it mate, I'm not blind! But he's got to help us, see." He turned back to Josh and poked a finger in his chest. "So what are you planning to do, young man? Eh?"

"Well…" said Josh, clearing his throat and noticing that more people had downed tools and edged their way forward to listen, "I'm going to rescue my parents and help you overthrow Machin," he called out in a cracked voice. To his surprise, the words started to flow. "We can win this thing, you know!" he cried. "We've already got Maxtrader on our side." They seemed confused by that bit, so he tried another tack. "After all, we're pirates! And we've got the great Matilda behind us. The future will not be Machin!" The mob broke into cheers, and the elderly spokesman patted him on the shoulder. "I told you the Guardian would help us," he said, "so let's get back to work. Otherwise, we won't get this thing finished by nightfall."

"Well done on the speech!" Megs whispered in his ear. "You're getting good at this stuff!"

Admiration glistened in her eyes. She meant it!

Away to their right, a young rebel officer waited for them at the entrance to the caves. He didn't look like a soldier – he had a black velvet jacket and a red scarf, and he wore his cap at a jaunty angle. He saluted in a light-hearted way and led them through a narrow archway in the rocks into a wide, dank circular chamber with tunnels leading off in all directions. The officer pointed to one of the tunnels. "I'm Adrian," he said. "I used to be an estate agent. Watch your step. The ground's uneven and it's quite dark in places. I wouldn't say that if I was trying to sell the place, mind you."

"Where are we going?" asked Josh.

"Headquarters," explained the officer. They had to speak in whispers now as the sound echoed in the eerie silence underground. "Things have got worse here recently," he explained. "Fleck's in charge now."

Josh kept walking. He tried to brush the thought of Fleck from his mind.

"Yes," Adrian continued. "They've got two thousand prisoners now, all working night and day in slave camps on the northwest headland. Can you imagine? A few days ago, they massacred a hundred or so in a test run of the oblivion bomb. That dampened some spirits, I can tell you."

They were deep underground now and wove their way downwards through a network of dimly lit interconnected tunnels. "It's some place, this," observed Adrian. "Even if a few of them managed to penetrate the outer defences, there are mines and booby traps all over the place. They'd suffer a lot of casualties before they smoked us out."

Josh heard a dry cough from Sandy's dad behind, feeling his way forward like a gorilla, in a permanent stoop. "Perhaps that's what they would do," he said, "Smoke us out."

They continued in silence for a bit.

"When will the bomb be ready?" asked Josh.

"Don't know," said Adrian. "There are lots of laboratories, and lots of scientists. All distilling oblivion, I suppose. Then they've got a vast construction site where more prisoners are employed excavating and cementing the base for the oblivion gun. What more can I tell you?"

"How many are there?" asked Josh. "Enemy soldiers, I mean?"

"Fighting forces? Well, there's the guards; about a thousand of them. They patrol the barbed wire perimeter of the prison camp. Then there's the two thousand regular soldiers. They spend their time drilling and practising their shooting skills on rabbits, blades of grass or the occasional prisoner who strays into their line of vision. I don't know what they'd be like as a fighting force. We'd better keep our voices down now. You are about to enter rebel headquarters."

In a well-lit cavern a long way below ground, they were introduced to the general's deputy, a tall, swarthy pirate with a scar on one cheek and a black eye-patch. He stood in the centre of a bare circular cavern, behind a long trestle table. One or two orderlies passed in and out with messages from time to time.

"The people, they ask me how things, they are going," he explained in a deep, guttural voice with a pronounced southern-piratical accent. "And I say things, they are going bad. Provisions they are low. The morale is low. We lose seventy peoples in the last bamboozle. Seventy out of a total numeration of two hundred and ninety."

"Why are you building a wall?" asked Josh.

The deputy turned to him. "Is the boy with the stone! Welcome! Welcome!" he said, extending a rough hand to greet him. "The enemy, he have discover where are we hiding. And so we must to stop him from enter the grottes."

"He means caves," whispered Sandy.

An orderly rushed in, narrowly escaping collision with two bats crossing the cavern from opposite directions.

"Advance warning, Ma'am. The enemy are planning to attack tonight."

More pirates poured into the cavern, jostling each other and talking about what they had just seen and heard.

"Call everyone into the caves now," said a clear, firm voice.

Everyone went quiet and looked round as an elderly gentleman in military uniform stepped into view.

"The general," whispered Sandy.

Josh stared at the kindly old man whose blue eyes darted round the cavern with lively interest. He didn't look like the famous general who'd once saved the island at the battle of 'The Last Resort'. With his grey whiskers and shambling gait, he looked more like a friendly badger. He walked towards the trestle table and spoke to his deputy. Then he turned and exchanged whispered words with the orderly, who raced back up the tunnel to convey the command to the men working on the wall.

The general coughed and everyone went silent again. "You did a great job with that wall," he said, casting his gaze around the room. "It will do for our first line of defence, but we can't hold out there for long. We don't have enough men to spare. We can't spare any of you, in fact. You are the precious backbone of our little island, the people who risked their lives to save it from the wreckage of Machin."

He stopped and waved above his head a copy of *The Daily Trumpeter*. "Some of you may be familiar with this..." he hesitated... "newspaper." Friendly laughter echoed round the cavern. "Some of Machin's generals – the old sort, the ones that can read, read this newspaper every day. They will be shocked to learn that this newspaper is now on our side!" Everyone cheered. "So don't be surprised, gentlemen, if any time soon, one of these generals appears at the entrance to our cave, begging permission to join us!" More cheers. The general lowered his voice. "Until that time comes, we will take to the caves and we will make it very difficult for the enemy to enter. And if they overcome the first obstacle, they will encounter more obstacles further down each tunnel until we reach the mist. And then, who knows! For the moment, you know what to do. You've practised it before. The men I've selected will defend the wall so long as it's safe to do so, and then join the rest of us in the caves."

Josh stood beside Sandy and Megs in the centre of the cavern while pirates ran past in all directions, hurrying to their stations. Bertie gave a good-natured shrug and followed Sandy's dad to join the men defending the wall.

At that moment, the general spotted them. "Ah, Josh. That's right isn't it? Josh?" The general clasped his hand warmly in his own two hands. "And you must be Megs. I've heard a lot about both of you. I know Sandy, of course. I call him my man of the mist. Well, we may have need of your skills if we're forced to take refuge there."

Chapter Fourteen

The cavern swarmed with rebel soldiers, talking in hushed tones, checking their equipment or standing around staring into their memories and waiting for their next orders. Josh heard groans from the emergency ward somewhere in a tunnel to his left. The deputy sat at the long trestle table, his scarred face sagging with worry and lack of sleep.

"Have you heard anything on your radio?" the general asked. "How many this time?"

"Is no many, my general;" he replied, "a diversion. More is coming very nextly."

"Good. Then we're safe here for the moment."

A breathless orderly raced into the cavern, skidding to a halt when he saw the general. "They are approaching in numbers, sir," he panted.

"How far away?" asked the general.

"Maybe a mile. They've got more helicopters."

The general nodded. "That's all we needed to know. We'd better abandon our defence of the wall soon and lure the enemy into the tunnels. That gives us more points to defend but we should be able to hold them off for a while."

Amid the noise of pirates shouting to one another and soldiers racing in and out of the crowded cavern, it took Josh some time to notice that the firing had stopped. The realisation spread round the chamber and strident voices sank to a questioning whisper. Eyes turned towards the trestle table where the general stood talking with his deputy. Josh noticed gloom in the eyes of some pirates who thought the silence meant surrender.

Bertie wiped dust and sweat from his round face as he emerged from the tunnel. A cheer went up as Sandy's dad followed him into the room. Because of his size and the fact that he was a colonist fighting on the pirate side, the men in that room regarded him as a hero.

"What's happening now?" Josh asked Bertie.

Bertie looked vaguely pleased with himself. "We gave a good account of ourselves," he said, "but they're regrouping." He glanced at the general. "I hope there's a plan B," he added, "because we can't hold them off for much longer."

Josh found a chair at the end of the trestle table and sat head in hands. He remembered what he'd said about helping them overthrow Machin. Brave words! 'The great Matilda's behind us.' That's what he'd said. But where? And what could she do? In a little while, thousands of enemy troops would come swarming over the plain, over the dried- up bed of the river Oblivion, to smoke them out of their caves. That's what they'd do, of course. Whatever obstacles the rebel forces erected, Machin's armies would smoke them out in the end – unless they escaped through the mist, and only he and Sandy had so far managed to do that.

"I've been thinking," said a slow voice at his shoulder. Sandy came and sat beside him at the trestle table. The bench creaked under his added weight.

Josh stared at the table.

"You know that river?" Sandy continued in thoughtful monotone. "It's dried up. But if it wasn't dried up…"

"Yes, but it is, so that's that!"

"But if it wasn't – say if it wasn't – if the waters from the lake flowed into the river like they ought to be flowing, then those armies wouldn't be able to cross the plain."

Josh turned on his friend. "Look Sandy, is there a point to all this?"

"Well, the lake's dried up too."

Josh threw up his hands in desperation. "Exactly!"

"But you ought to ask yourself why it's dried up. It's because of the mist. All the waters of that lake have gone into the mist."

"And?"

"Well, Matilda made that mist, didn't she? That's what you pirates believe. She made it to stop that prince from getting his hands on that little red flower."

Josh had heard enough. He stood up. "Look, Sandy! In case you hadn't noticed, we're in the middle of a war."

Sandy pulled him down again. His eyes bulged like a bullfrog's. "I'm trying to tell you something important, Josh," he said. "The mist isn't needed any more. Machin's already got his hands on that flower. Do you believe in Matilda, or what? You said yourself that she'll help us so why don't you ask her? Ask her to dissolve the mist. Isn't that why you've got that stone thing? Isn't that what Guardians are for?"

Josh turned to his friend. "I don't know, Sandy. I really don't know. Let me think about this."

"I was just going to say–"

"Well, don't. Don't say any more. You've made your point, and it's a good one. Just let me think."

"It may not work," said Sandy as he moved away "But are you more afraid of looking silly or looking dead?"

"Just let me think!"

He screwed his eyes shut, until the colours shifted from orange to red to black and the noise in the crowded room seemed as distant as nails scratching on glass. He thought about Matilda and the river of Oblivion and the lake but, instead of those images, another image came to mind.

He remembered that girl again, in a pink cardigan and a frilly, white blouse done up to her neck; Lavinia! The man she was speaking to had turned round so that Josh could see his boxer's broken nose and his dark, resentful eyes. He sounded angry:

"You set me up, girl! You had this planned all along."

She had played the man like a fish. She had that ability. You could see it in her eyes.

"What are you asking me to do?"

"Release the boy's parents from gaol. Stage an escape. Whatever. Tell them they are free to go home."

Josh felt a lightening of the heart. He remembered that Lavinia had done what she had promised to do. She'd fulfilled her part of the bargain. He blinked a few times and his gaze returned to the cavern. Pirate soldiers filled the crowded space, talking in calm voices, organising and making plans. He got up and walked over to his friend.

"Come on, Sandy. Let's go."

Sandy looked confused. "Go where?"

"To the lake, of course! I'm going to speak to Matilda and rescue my parents."

It was Sandy's turn to look worried. "Look, Josh, you've got this all wrong. I never said anything about your parents. We don't know where they are for a start and, anyway, that's for later."

"Yes, later." Josh turned to his friend. "Trust me, Sandy. I know what I'm doing. We have to get to that lake because that's where I have my best chance of speaking to Matilda."

"But why the lake? Why not here and now?"

"Because it's a sacred lake, right? Whatever you call it – magic – I dunno – the lake is close to the centre of things. It wouldn't work here, believe me. Let's get to that lake. And after? Well, we'll see."

He found the general speaking to Dame Mirabella. Megs was with them.

Josh waited his turn. If you're going to say something that sounds silly, he thought, best get it over with fast.

The general noticed him at last. "You look as if you've got something important to tell me," he said.

"I have to go to the lake and ask Matilda to dissolve the mist," said Josh, in as sensible a voice as he could muster.

He stopped, expecting the general to laugh or dismiss him, but the old man just bent his head and listened, so Josh blundered on. "The waters of the mist will fall into the sacred lake and the river will flow again and flood the plain." The general still said nothing, so he concluded lamely, "So that's why I have to go the lake. And Sandy's coming with me."

The general peered upwards at an imaginary mist. He let the mist slip through his fingers into an imaginary lake and slowly shook his head in wonder.

"He sounds a bit weird sometimes," said Megs.

The general examined him closely. "Does he? Does he?" he asked. "I'm not a pirate, you see, and sometimes their ideas strike me as a bit alternative. But he's the Guardian, isn't he? So, you never know." He turned to Josh. "Tell me exactly what you need to do."

"I just need to get to that lake."

The general nodded again, several times. "But you know where the lake is?"

"I suppose it's in the centre of the mist."

"That's right. Well, it can't do any harm, I suppose, and it may do us all a lot of good. And you'll have Sandy with you. He's the man of the mist. Adrian will show you the way."

"I'm coming too," said Megs. She clenched her jaw and stared at the general – halfway between obstinacy and tears.

The old man slowly shook his head. "I can't spare you, Megs." He put his arm over her shoulder. "Now these boys are protected against the mist but, in your case, it might kill you. I don't think I could bear that responsibility. I hope you understand?"

Megs quietly nodded and allowed the general to lead her away. She turned to Josh as she walked off. "I'm not as dumb as you think," she said. "I can listen when people explain things properly. Good luck with your mist."

The enemy firing had already started again as Josh and Sandy followed their guide down the long narrow tunnel which wound its way eastward under the mist. Josh marvelled at the workmanship of the tunnel, with bright lights set in the walls at intervals and shafts cut into the rocky ceiling, providing misty air from a hundred feet above their heads. They could easily walk upright along the sloping floor and they passed through several circular chambers where they could gather in one space instead of following in single file.

"This tunnel was once the most important tunnel of them all," explained Adrian. "Pirates built it in the days before the mist. It leads out near the sacred lake. In fact, we are walking towards what used to be the entrance." He tapped the solid walls. "Stonework, most of it; they built well in those days."

They had been travelling downhill for about an hour now and Josh felt a layer of dirt and moisture forming on his skin from the cold, dank stones above his head.

Adrian pointed to a circle of light at the bottom of the slope. "That's where the tunnel ends," he explained. They hurried after him and soon found themselves in a cavern, as spacious as the one they left at the start of their journey.

"I have to leave you chaps now," said Adrian. He pointed to a low archway in the wall facing them where two stone steps led upwards into the darkness. "Those steps will take you into the mist. Once you get through that arch, hold on to the metal handrail and you should be safe enough." He turned to Josh. "Now, you know what you have to do?"

"Just keep going east until I come to the lake?"

"That's right."

"I've got my torch," said Sandy, "and my compass in case we lose our way."

"Good," said Adrian, with a smile. "I'm sure those implements will be useful. Good luck on your journey." He gave a wave and hurried off.

Sandy grasped the metal rail and started to climb, with Josh just behind. "Never mind the mist!" Sandy cried. "If you think about it logically, it can't harm us, unlike the enemy we've left behind."

Josh didn't feel in the mood for logic. He just climbed. Soon he could see a small circle of grey light above his head and then Sandy's face peering down at him.

He climbed out into a misty wall – much thicker than anything he remembered from before. It entered his lungs like porridge, viscous and clinging. He reached for the stone and squeezed it, feeling the strength of the mist fall away like a veil.

"The mist is in the mind," said Sandy, sitting down on a lump of rock. "If you think about it, it's there."

"Yes, Sandy. Can we get moving?"

"Or not there," said Sandy. "What I mean is that the mist doesn't really exist. So..."

"Shut up, Sandy!"

"Ok," said Sandy. "I was just going to add..."

"Well, don't."

"Ok."

Josh stepped back into a patch of soft mud. "Damn. I'm sinking! Don't just stand there. Do something!"

He had already sunk up to his knees, and it took all Sandy's strength to pull him out, like a cork from a bottle.

"That's what I was going to add," said Sandy.

"Sorry, I should have listened," said Josh. "Let's get moving."

Sandy led the way eastward. They didn't find it as easy, cutting through the central core of the mist, as when they'd skirted it before. Sandy held his compass out in front of him. After some patient searching, he shone his torch on a line of stepping-stones heading east across a swamp. They had to pick their way over the stones in the misty darkness until they stumbled onto a straight gravel path. It was not long before they saw lights in the distance – faint shimmering lights strung out in a circle that defined the edges of the lake.

Josh walked towards the lights with increasing confidence until he stumbled upon the lake. Not a ripple stirred its flat surface. He reached down and dipped a long stick in the water. "We guessed right," he said. "It's only a few inches deep."

"What happens next?" asked Sandy.

"Sh!"

He reached into his pouch for the stone. Nothing. No reaction. The stone didn't even glow.

Feeling extremely foolish, he called out in an uncertain voice, "I call upon Matilda to dissolve the mist!"

"Maybe she can't hear you," said Sandy.

Josh rounded on his friend. "Maybe it would be better if you went and sat under that tree. I need to concentrate."

Sandy nodded and wandered off. "I'll sit and watch," he said. "You can have my torch."

Josh shouted into the mist. He waited. Still no answer and no sign of any movement. He tried again, louder, gripping his stone and shining Sandy's torch on the water. "I call upon Matilda!"

He examined his stone. It emitted a faint orange glow, but he couldn't feel Matilda's presence. And shouting into the mist just seemed useless and silly. Yet, when he went over Sandy's logic in his mind, it surely made sense. Matilda created the mist in order to protect them; now their safety depended on its removal. "Please, Matilda," he said in a quiet voice, squeezing his stone until his fingers ached, "I know you're here. Please dissolve your mist and save us."

Just then a tiny drop of rain landed on his forehead. He looked up and felt another raindrop splash on the end of his nose; then another and another. Then, far away, he heard the crash of thunder, followed by another crash directly overhead. Then a flash of lightning streaked across the sky, and raindrops came pelting down, hitting the grass around him like bullets and bending the trees and soaking him to the skin.

He groped around and found Sandy, still sitting under his tree.

"What was all that about?" asked Sandy. "I saw you doing a lot of shouting."

"Didn't you see anything?"

"I saw the lightning. Listen, we'd better get onto higher ground. The water's lapping round our feet."

"Can you hear anything?"

"Only the sound of a storm. Let's go!"

They raced up the nearest slope that took them a few metres above the water. "She listened," cried Josh in wonder. "Can't you see how the mist is beginning to lighten?" He looked down at the waters flowing towards his feet. "What happens now? Do you think we'll drown?"

At that moment, they both heard a crashing sound away to their west.

"I think we'll be safe," said Sandy. "The water's stopped rising. If anything, it's starting to recede."

"That must have been the noise that we just heard," agreed Josh. "She's unblocked the lake. The water's flowing west into the river of Oblivion." He punched the air with his fist. "We've done it! We've flooded the plain! Our friends are safe!"

CHAPTER FIFTEEN

Lavinia walked towards the sound of a rhinoceros being let loose in her stepdad's bedroom. She stood on the threshold, doing up the top button of her blouse as she watched the maid, Maria, squeal and hop around on her stubby legs, dodging furniture being hurled at the walls. She took a deep breath and waited.

As soon as he spotted her, her stepdad came raging towards her, his voice thick with menace. "The boy's parents have escaped. And you don't know where they are, of course." He mimicked her girlie tone of voice. "Explain that away, if you can!"

Lavinia struggled to keep her voice steady. "Saintly," she said.

Another chair hit the wall. Another hop and squeal from Maria. "Shut your noise, woman," he bellowed. Again, he bore down on his stepdaughter and stood there studying her with cold, hard eyes. "It's strange, isn't it?" he mused, "the way accidents seem to happen round you. And it's never your fault, is it?" – his tone had an edge to it – "You're just a fat slug worming your way into my favour–"

"Saintly," she repeated.

"Shut up, girl, did I ask you to speak?" His hands were on her throat. "Did I ask you? You'll speak when you're asked to speak." He pushed her away so that she nearly toppled over.

"Saintly," she persisted.

He raised his hand to slap her face and froze in mid-air. "And stop repeating that name," he shouted. "Speak when you're spoken to!" He raised his hand again.

She didn't budge. "I'm just giving you facts," she stated. "Saintly released the boy's parents from gaol. Saintly warned off the pirate bankers. Saintly tipped off Draco. All facts. You asked me to be your eyes and ears. Now I'm just your fat Slug who can't do anything right." Her eyes watered with artificial tears.

She'd aroused his interest. He opened his mouth, preparing to launch into another attack, but she cut in quickly. "Think it out, Daddy. Who has the power to free the boy's parents from gaol? Do you think I have the power? I don't even have the power to leave this house! But do I complain? I promised to stick by your side and that's what I've always done." Another burst of manufactured tears.

"So why didn't you warn me about his plan?"

She tried the little girl eyes. "I didn't know."

He stopped in his tracks. "For goodness sake, girl," he exploded. "You spin this whole ridiculous story about Saintly and then you tell me you know nothing about it!"

"Common sense, Daddy," she reasoned. "Who else had the power to release them? Do you think any of the guards would dare move without his say-so? Besides…"

He was calming down now, beginning to listen intently. "Besides what?"

"I already suspected him because of the way he warned those bankers. He took a shed load of money from them – as a bribe, I suppose. It's probably still there in his right-hand jacket pocket".

The detail intrigued him, but again his eyes wavered as doubts crept in. "But you didn't think to tell me?"

"I told you about Draco," she said quickly, eager to smooth over the weak point in her story, "and I would have told you about the bankers too, but it was too late. It wouldn't have done any good and I knew you wouldn't believe me."

"Well, maybe I should start believing you," he said in a dangerously reasonable voice.

His next question came like the stab of a knife below the ribs. "So how did you know about the bankers?"

"How did I know?"

"You heard me."

"I heard him talking to Draco."

"Draco's dead. You knew that, didn't you? Very convenient so far as your story is concerned."

Lavinia played her last card. She stared at the ground and asked in a quiet voice. "Look, Daddy, can I go now?"

He didn't say anything. A good sign. The question had caught him off guard. She gave him another dose of the little girl eyes. "I mean it's obvious that you don't believe me whatever I say, even though I'm the only person who's really trying to help you, but it just doesn't work because you don't want to be helped, not by me at any rate, so you'd be much better off without me…"

Her sobbing fit was interrupted by Maria, who'd slipped away while this conversation was taking place. Reginald Machin looked up. "Yes, Maria?"

"Saintly's at the door, sir."

He looked at his stepdaughter. His eyes told her he didn't know what to do. He really didn't know what to do!

"Lavinia?"

"Yes."

He'd actually spoken her name in a nice way. She risked putting a hand on his arm and noticed that he didn't shrug it off. "Daddy," she said in her little girl voice, "I know you're the politician and all that, but do you think that's a good step – I mean at the moment, when you are just getting all your plans sorted? You need Saintly because he – I dunno," – she waved her hands vaguely in the air – "he runs the secret service and all that stuff. Why not just behave like nothing's happened and add him to your mantelpiece collection when you no longer need him?"

She could tell he liked the idea. He wore that glassy stare that usually preceded some act of manic brutality. "And the boy's parents," he said in a far-away voice. "I suppose it's not such a bad idea to let them escape. They can't have left the island. Probably just walked back to their own house. It's the only place they could go. And the boy's not far away. He's joined the rebel forces, I hear. I bet he plans to rescue them! Just the sort of heroic nonsense he's capable of. Find the parents, set a trap for the boy – I like it!"

"Yes, Daddy!" *She wanted to scream.*

"Lavinia! I'm beginning to wonder what I'd do without you."

"Thank you, Daddy!" *Grateful smile.*

"But I've just had an even better idea!" A slow, predatory grin spread over his face. "You'll like this one, Lavinia."

"Yes, Daddy." Lavinia's jaw ached with the effort to dissemble.

"Set a trap, yes. But, just to be on the safe side, why not remove the cheese? You haven't seen our basements, have you, Lavinia? That's where we keep our most important prisoners – the ones we intend to execute. I'll have a cell prepared for them straightaway."

"Yes, Daddy." *She had to warn the boy's parents, but there was no time!*

Chapter Sixteen

Josh sat beside Sandy at the top of the slope watching the mist fall in a steady drizzle over the trees, over the surrounding hills and over the lake, for miles around, letting tiny patches of sunlight seep through. Most of the mist funnelled into the lake. Josh saw the surface rise and fall like the overflow from a basin after you'd removed the plug. The waters had drowned the lights on the western rim and thundered on in a wide sweep, narrowing slightly in the distance as they settled into the dried-up bed of the river Oblivion. Soon more water pushing from behind caused the river to overflow its banks and the flood raced on westward in a wide, unstoppable flow. Ancient trees that had died from lack of contact with the sun cracked and toppled in its path. The sound of rushing waters rang in his ears. Somewhere out of sight those waters would soon reach that wide, grassy plain which used to be called 'the edge of the world'.

Not anymore! To left and right of him, the view lightened by the minute. He imagined the rebels in that cavern, hearing the waters thundering across the plain. The torrent skirted the higher ground to the south where the tunnels had their outlets. But no army could cross the central plain. Only helicopters could reach the caves now.

"Do you think the harvest is flooded?" asked Sandy.

Josh gave a guilty start. "Yea," he said. Strange that he'd never given that a thought.

"The army will be safe now," said Sandy, "from that side of the island, at least."

Josh's eyes switched to the east. Of course! Without the mist, troops could move westward with ease. He pictured them marching down that lane past his parents' house.

"Do you think we should go now?" asked Sandy.

"Go where?"

"Back to the caves. And you need to change your clothes."

Josh realised his clothes were sodden and he'd started to shiver. He stood up and jumped and flapped his arms around.

"What are you doing?"

"Getting warm."

He stopped his exercises and sat down again. "Why would my parents stay in the house?" he asked. "I mean, even with that mist, I still think they'd try to battle through somehow rather than risk getting caught by the CP. But the mist has gone now. Imagine it! People will be swarming past their house soon. Surely, they'd want to be the first to get away?"

Sandy fiddled with his compass. "Unless they were trapped," he said.

"I thought about that, but if they were trapped, they'd be back in prison by now."

Sandy shook his head. "Not if the trap was meant for you. That's what they'd do, isn't it; use your parents as hostages?"

Josh got up. He knew Sandy could be right. "Let's go," he said.

Sandy hadn't moved. "Go where?" he asked.

"To the house, of course! Come on! What are you doing?"

"Thinking," said Sandy.

"But the house is only a mile away. It's obvious! If we wait, there could be troops marching all over the place."

Sandy put his compass back in his pocket and looked up. "Why are you waving your arms around like that?" he asked. "We need to speak to the general. He can help us. He's got troops to spare now. We can't just walk into a trap. That's no use to your parents."

Josh knew that he'd go alone if need be, but it would be better with Sandy at his side. "What if we go just a little way?" he asked. "Up to that silver birch tree, remember? At least we can scan the house with your binoculars and find out what we're up against." Sandy opened his mouth to speak but Josh interrupted him. "Look, there's no time. If we wait till the mist is cleared, the enemy will be expecting us."

"They're probably expecting us now," said Sandy, but he got up. "I'll go with you as far as that tree," he said.

As they made their way through the thick undergrowth, the mist still hung round them. Grey wisps swirled around their feet and were sucked into the lake, to be replaced by fresh mist tumbling from above. But they could see a sharp diagonal line in the distance where the grey mist ended, and the blue sky began.

"There's the tree," said Sandy.

They'd reached the silver birch tree where they'd stopped on their outward journey. From there they could see the house. Josh pointed excitedly at the lights shining through the upstairs, living-room window. "My parents," he cried. "They must be in the house!"

"What did you expect?" asked Sandy.

"I didn't know," he admitted. "They could have gone somewhere else or been captured and taken back to prison. At least I know where they are! I know it! Let's go on."

"But you said–"

"I know, but it's safe to go a little further. Nobody else is around yet."

"Yet."

"Please!" Josh started walking towards the house. He didn't look round, but he heard Sandy sigh and stand up.

"Wait for me!" he said, putting his rucksack back on his shoulder.

It didn't take them long to reach a clump of bushes just beyond the rickety white gate leading into the back garden. They threw themselves down in the long grass, under the cover of the bushes, and stared at the house. Josh felt a pang of nostalgia, seeing the neglected, long grass and the three laden apple trees in the far-right corner of the lawn. "Can you see anything?" he asked.

Sandy stared through his binoculars. "Nothing. Just lights in your living room, but I could see those without my binoculars. What can you see?"

"Well, obviously the garden's in a mess but they haven't had time to clear it up yet."

"Yea, but what's changed?"

"Nothing. Except–" Josh stared at the back door. "The door's open. My mum never leaves the back door open. Never. She says the mist gives her the creeps."

Sandy picked up his binoculars again and trained them on the upstairs room. "I still can't see your parents, but I can see someone standing at the window. That's strange. It's someone we know. Take a look."

Josh had a queasy sensation in his stomach. He trained the binoculars on the living room window and quickly passed them back. "It's the Cat Lady," he said.

"I know."

Sandy trained his binoculars on the lane behind the house.

"What are you doing?" Josh asked.

"They'd need more than one person to guard the house," said Sandy "but I can't see anyone." He adjusted the lenses. "That's where they are," he said, passing the binoculars to Josh. "Over there. Two white vans. They are waiting for a sign from the Cat

Lady, I suppose. They're keeping out of sight because you're not supposed to know they're there. There must be about twenty men in those white vans. As soon we enter the house, they'll nab us."

"What if we don't enter?" said Josh. He pointed to a thin line of bushes to the right of the garden. "There's just rocks beyond that," he said. "It's a sharp drop down to the sea, but if we keep close to those bushes we can get round that way and slip in through the back door."

Sandy looked at his friend. "Are you mad?" he asked. He picked up the binoculars again. "The Cat Lady's expecting you. She keeps coming to the window and looking in our direction."

"She can't see us. Anyway, how would she know we're coming?"

"A spy," said Sandy in his flat voice. "My dad said there's a spy in the rebel army; probably someone with a relative in prison. I mean, if a member of your family was caught by Fleck, wouldn't you want to do anything – I mean, anything – to get them free?"

"Like I'm doing now," said Josh.

"We can't stay here forever," said Sandy.

"What if we lure her into the garden?"

Sandy sat up. "I've seen enough. Let's go back and get help."

"Seriously, Sandy; think it out. The men in that van can't see the garden from there. If we can catch her at the back door and stop her from making a noise – we can slip into the house without being seen."

"I think we should go back."

"If we go back, she'll spot us anyway." Josh pointed at the flat ground they had crossed in order to reach the cover of the bushes. "That's the way we came," he said. "We managed it once because she wasn't looking – or we think she wasn't – but as soon we go back that way, those men will come after us."

Sandy looked back the way they had come. He looked back at the house again. He seemed to be coming round to the idea. "I suppose we could overpower her," he said. "I've got my pistol."

"Are you crazy? They'd hear it. Have you got your rope?"

"Yea."

"I'll lure her into the open and you grab her from behind, right?"

"Right." Sandy fumbled around for something in his rucksack.

Josh remembered the games he used to play. He knew the perfect way to approach the house without being seen. Before Sandy could change his mind, he set off to his right on hands and knees, under the cover of the bushes. After a while, he heard Sandy puffing along behind him. Where these bushes ended and the cliffs began, another line of bushes marked the southern border of the garden. Under the cover of these bushes, they edged their way to within a few yards of the back door.

Josh stopped to get his breath back. He lay there panting, going through the plan in his head. What if she didn't come to the door? What if she reached for her phone? What if she had a gun? What if she screamed and alerted those men in the van? What if they couldn't overpower her? What if she had an accomplice in the house?

He signalled to Sandy, who slowly got up and flattened himself against the wall of the house, inching forward until he came to rest in a crouching position behind the back door.

The Cat Lady had come to the window. Had she heard something? She poked her head out and looked around. He saw her sharp, inquisitive face, scanning the garden up and down. Then she stuck her head in again.

He grasped a pebble in his hand, ran out in front of the house and tossed it at the window. Then he raced and hid in the open doorway. Strange. He'd thrown the pebble hard enough but he'd failed to break the window. The noise must have been enough to catch her attention. He couldn't see her from the doorway.

"What's she doing?" he whispered.

"She's looking down. Sh!"

He heard the living room door open and feet padding down the stairs. He moved away from the door and waited. He heard a flurry of movement. She'd reached the landing. Had she stopped? No. He heard her mutter something and set off again. Her footsteps thundered down the stairs. He could see her. She almost tumbled into his arms. He felt her soft arms and a whiff of scent. Then she righted herself and a slow smile spread across her face. "Ah, Josh…!"

Her face lurched backwards as Sandy's strong arm grabbed her by the neck from behind. Before she could struggle, his other arm reached round and sprayed something down her throat. Her eyes widened. "What a lovely smell!" she sighed, flopping to the ground in a graceful heap.

"What did you do, Sandy?"

Sandy knelt over the fallen body. He cringed, as if expecting a telling off. "Sorry, Plan B. I didn't think the other plan would work. That was 'Snort.' I kept some in my rucksack. I got it from one of the kids at school, just in case. Don't tell my dad."

"That's the oblivion juice. What have you done, Sandy? Have you killed her?"

"No, she'll come round in a few minutes."

"What are you doing now?"

"I'm trying to find her phone and her keys – ah! Here!"

"Where's the rope?"

"Here."

"We'd better stuff something in her mouth, tie her up and drag her inside."

Josh looked at Sandy. "Can you deal with her for the moment?" he asked.

Sandy nodded.

"Then, I'll just run upstairs. That's probably where they are."

Josh raced up the stairs to the sitting room. Where else could they be? He found the room stripped bare, the carpet ripped away, just a few red-patterned patches sticking to the floor. Choking with desperation, he rushed up to their bedroom and his own attic bedroom next door. Both rooms had been trashed, but junk-strewn floors and cupboard doors ripped from their hinges left no room to hide. Had he missed something downstairs? The kitchen, maybe? Of course, they could be in the kitchen! He dashed down the stairs, casting a quick glance through the porthole window overlooking the front door.

One glance was enough. The white van doors had opened, spilling their occupants out onto the lane.

He found Sandy dragging his captive by the shoulders into the bare kitchen. Sandy lowered her head to the floor. "She's beginning to talk," he said, straightening up. "She says it's a trap. She says Machin's taken them. She says–"

"Don't say any more, Sandy. Please! Those men have left their vans. They're heading for the house. Let's go!"

CHAPTER SEVENTEEN

In the absence of her stepdad, Lavinia ate dinner alone. She didn't feel like speaking to anyone this evening. She'd broken her promise and let the boy down. His parents would have been better off if she'd never meddled in the first place. But moping didn't help. She couldn't afford to relax her guard. She had to know what her dad was up to at any moment of the day. He controlled the news, so she was forced to watch it. She dimmed the lights and sat in the darkened room.

To her surprise, the news this evening was devoted to the mist. It had gone! Billy Swagger welcomed the event as a miracle. Did it mean that the earth wasn't flat after all? No, it simply meant that the boundary had been pushed westward, leaving more land for colonists to explore. Then a few pirates were interviewed – though their faces were obscured – ascribing the miracle to their young Guardian, whose actions had been prophesied in the *Piratica*. She eased into her chair. That kid had done what nobody thought was possible.

The fearless reporter gave a brief run up to the promised interview with Reginald Machin. Although the western part of Colony Island was barred to journalists, much of its central plain was known to be flooded. How had this affected the fields of little, red oblivion flowers due to be harvested? And how would this affect the production of the dreaded oblivion weapon? These were questions that our fearless reporter would be putting to Reginald Machin.

The camera lens widened to show her stepdad standing on the cliff top above Greystones harbour on Discovery Island.

"He looks mad," she thought, "stark staring mad; down to his last marble."

"Good afternoon," said the young representative of *Daily Update*. "I'm Jeremy Stirfry. Quite a mouthful, I'm afraid. I expect our viewers would like to know what you are doing over here on Discovery Island."

Her stepdad struck up a pose, heroic and windswept, standing on a rock staring out to sea. His face filled the screen. "I am a man of peace," he said.

That's it, thought Lavinia. He must have declared war on someone.

"But sometimes when the security of one's own little island is at stake, one is forced to act," – he thumped his fist into the palm of his hand – "and to act again and again!"

"Yes, indeed," agreed Jeremy Stirfry. She noticed he'd retreated a few paces.

"Today, we have come to the aid of our dear friends in Discovery Island whose oppressive government launched an attack on us."

"They shot down one of your helicopters," suggested Jeremy Stirfry.

Her stepdad glared. "As I was saying, they launched an attack on us."

"For violating their airspace," continued Jeremy Stirfry, "after you were given several warnings." He smiled at Reginald Machin, retreating well out of arm's reach. "Sorry, I thought I'd better get that straight for the benefit of our viewers."

Her stepdad brushed the point aside with a flap of his hand. "The point I would like to make absolutely clear, if you would be kind enough to let me speak–"

"Yes, indeed," said Jeremy Stirfry.

"Is that we in our little island are not afraid to defend our rights. We will go to any lengths, we will even use weapons-of-mass-destruction," – he said the last words at a gallop as if he were trying to swallow a hard-boiled egg, "to defend those rights. So let the government of Crown Colony beware – if they choose to carry on this vicious campaign of propaganda against us, aiding and abetting traitors within our society to overthrow our duly elected government."

"What's he on about?" she wondered. "Is he going to attack Crown Colony next?"

The voice ranted on. "I say, if they so choose, on their heads be it! Yes, we will let loose our weapons-of-mass-destruction."

"You mean the bomb? On their heads, you were saying? Have you actually got a bomb? Our understanding was that the harvest had been flooded."

Her stepdad stared at Jeremy Stirfry as if he'd failed to get the message. "What are you talking about? The bomb has been already been prepared. Of course we've got a bomb. Any number of bombs; oblivion bombs. Our soldiers, our helicopters are standing ready to defend our sacred land."

"And what about your own people? There are rumoured to be some elements that are not entirely happy with your style of government."

'Some elements!' She liked that.

"What elements?" He glared and jerked his head back like an angry swan. "My people are entirely happy with my government – apart from a few pirates who caused all the trouble in the first place. I was voted into office, I would have you remember."

"Yes, indeed, but what about the prison camps and the secret police – the 'CPs', I believe they're called?"

"Perfectly legitimate measures to secure the safety of the majority of good clean-living people of Colony Island."

"Yes, indeed."

"And stop saying 'yes, indeed'! I think this interview has gone on quite long enough." Suddenly the screen went black, followed by an apologetic announcement that Reginald Machin declined to answer further questions.

She shook her head in disgust and headed for her bedroom.

As soon as she opened her bedroom door, she saw Saintly's broad back blocking the end of her bed. She froze in the doorway. "Got an interesting tape here," he said, not bothering to look round. "I'll play it over for you if you want."

The cardboard box in his hands frightened her more than the tape. He had tipped out some of the contents onto her bed. How had he found her secret hiding-place? Any moment he would turn and see the fear in her face.

She took a deep breath and tried to sound casual. "I wonder why it took you so long! I suppose it must have been hard, doctoring that tape – cutting out all the incriminating bits about yourself."

He waved the tape above his back. "You think so? Judge for yourself. I think you'll find the results are quite juicy."

"I'm not interested." She bit her lip.

"No? I think Machin will be interested. Mind you, there's material in this box that will interest him even more. This boy, for instance. Your pin-up, is he?"

Without turning round, he held up the photo of the boy with the twinkling eyes. Anger and sadness fought for control of her face.

"I'll keep this, if you don't mind." He put it in his right-hand jacket pocket.

"So you're giving up," she said, trying her last card.

"Giving you up, more like." He chuckled.

"You've clearly thought it through. He'll kill me. That's obvious."

"Yea." His reaction held out no hope except she noticed that he still refused to look at her. "Get things back on track." His voice sounded more wistful than determined.

"Except they won't be."

He didn't answer. A good sign. She turned the card over, revealing her ace. "Anyway, I'll be off now, Saintly. You can use my room if you like. I'd lock the door if it makes you feel safer."

This time he did turn to face her. He gave an astonished laugh. "I must say, girl, you've got a nerve. I'll say that for you!"

The blood rushed to her head. "We've both got nerves, Saintly, except in my case they're connected to a brain. Do you think for one moment I trusted you to keep our little secret? My dad knows about you. He knows everything! I made sure of that!"

"He'll still kill you."

"He'll kill both of us." She paused. "At least, he'll certainly kill you, and if he has time to listen to your story before he puts a bullet through your brain, he'll kill me too."

Saintly stared at her with his hard eyes. She held his stare. She had the satisfaction of watching him stand up, shove the tape in his pocket and pick up the cardboard box. "I suppose it can wait," he said, stopping at the door. "Nice to have the evidence to use when I need it."

"Lavinia!!" The sound of her stepdad's voice echoed down the red-carpeted corridor.

He must have just returned from Discovery Island.

Saintly lingered in the doorway. His hesitation filled her with triumph. "Better wait in here for the moment," she advised him, taking control. "You never know when he's in one of his moods."

"Lavinia!!"

"I'll have to see what he wants. You can slip out the back way once I've got him engaged in conversation."

"I've been looking for you everywhere, Lavinia. Where have you been?"

Her stepdad's face was flushed, but not with anger – with triumph. He was pleased. What's more, he had come running down the corridor to share his pleasure with her!

"I've just taken Discovery Island," he said. "They surrendered without a fight. You know what this means?"

"It's good, isn't it?" She tried the little girl eyes.

"It's given us control of the Maxtrader steelworks. It sets us up nicely for the next step.

You know what the next step is, Slug?"

"The world?" she suggested.

He doubled up with laughter. It took him some time to recover. "The world!" he repeated, goading himself into another fit of laughter. "I like that." He shook his head. "No, the next step is Crown Colony – the crown of the Federation. Besides…"

She waited. The mad gleam had returned to his eyes. "I've given them an ultimatum."

"What's an ultimatum?"

"Be quiet! Don't interrupt! I shall say 'Hand over Magnus Maxtrader or I shall annihilate you with my oblivion bomb'."

"And then?"

"They'll hand him over, of course. Then I shall probably drop at least one bomb anyway."

"Why?" She hid her face.

"I don't know. Just to see what it can do." He grabbed her arm. "What's the matter, Slug? Don't you like the idea?"

"Yes but – I do, but - excuse me a moment –" Lavinia made a dash for the toilet. She stood there, gripping the wash basin in both hands, taking heavy, panting breaths. How was she supposed to like the idea of her mum and her granddad, not to mention thousands of other, innocent people, being destroyed by a psychopath prepared to drop a lethal bomb on them just 'to see what it can do'?

She flushed the toilet and turned on both taps, throwing cold water over her face, and walked back up the corridor. "Sorry, Daddy. Something I had for breakfast. I feel better now."

His eyes had gone cold. "Thinking about Mummy and Granddad? Not quite sure whose side you're on after all?"

She recoiled inwardly but brushed his paranoia aside like a nurse dealing with an awkward patient. "I'm on your side, Daddy. You know that. Listen, there's something more important that's worrying me. Saintly."

She had his attention. "What about him?"

"He's got a pistol."

He relaxed. "Oh that! He's always got a pistol."

"He's intending to use it on you."

He nodded. She could see from his smile that he already had Saintly marked down to die.

"Draco," he announced, "I'll speak to Draco."

"I thought Draco was dead."

"Did I say that? I changed my mind. I thought I might need him. Once he's dealt with Saintly he's earned the right to take over the CPs. Well done, Slug, for reminding me."

He strode off down the corridor.

Lavinia heaved an uneasy sigh. She still had to get that cardboard box and the tape.

"Lavinia!" He stopped in his stride and turned back.

"Yes, Dad?"

"The boy's parents. I've re-arrested them."

"Wonderful!" *How this hypocrisy made her face ache.* "So your trap worked? Did you manage to catch the boy?"

"Not quite, Slug."

"Oh dear!" She clenched her fists. *Try to sound more convincing. I must try.*

"Never mind. I think I'll execute his parents tomorrow. That will give us one less thing to worry about. Not that I am ever worried."

"Of course, Dad. I mean, of course not! Well, you know what I mean!" She thought longingly of the long-bladed kitchen knife that she would love to plant in his departing back.

CHAPTER EIGHTEEN

T wo hundred pirates crammed into the cavern and sat cross-legged on the mud floor or leaned against the walls, facing a screen erected on the long trestle table. A few got up when Josh entered the cavern and insisted on leaving him a space at the front with Sandy and Megs. He was their Guardian hero who'd caused the flood and saved their army, but he didn't feel like a hero. Nobody except Sandy knew about the failed rescue.

"Do you think he'll do it?" whispered Megs.

"Do what?" asked Josh, "The bomb? Sh!"

The general had appeared in the cavern with a small group of rebel soldiers who'd been busy sealing the main entrance. Sandy's father and Bertie were among them. The general said something to Dame Belladonna and looked at his watch. He stood by the screen and his eyes travelled round the expectant throng.

"It won't work," whispered Sandy. "You can't seal all the entrances. There are just too many of them. It's like Snort, remember? But a thousand times more concentrated! Fleck's not a fool. He'll release an explosive device to open up the caves first and then the gas will flow in. If you want to know what I think–"

"We don't," said Megs. "Everyone can hear you," she added in a whisper, "So shut up! Please!"

"Good news," the general announced. "If we survive the next few hours, as I'm sure we will, we'll soon be part of a victorious army. There's been an uprising nearby in Snake Cove. All those families that live in the northern suburbs and send their children to the Machin Academies – generals, businessmen, flat-earthers – are getting restive. There's no food in the shops; not since Magnus Maxtrader turned off the tap. And now I hear that one of the main army divisions has mutinied. General Hawkspoon has seized control of the airport. With the airport in our hands, and the promised aid of our neighbouring islands, the Machin regime is ripe for plucking."

Josh heard scattered cheers. He thought of his parents holed up in the chief minister's house. Maybe the rebel army would win this war after all and Machin would be toppled and then they'd all be safe. But his stomach told him things didn't work that way – not with a mad dictator like Machin.

The general was still speaking. "Hawkspoon's sending a troop ship to pick us up," he continued. "Not now, of course, but soon, very soon, when all this is over." He waved a hand at the screen which crackled into life.

The reporter's handsome features came into focus. You could tell from his furrowed eyebrows and his firm jaw that he'd got some serious news to impart and he thought he looked good on camera. "Breaking news from Colony Island," he announced. "The rebellion will soon be at an end. Reginald Machin has announced that a team of 300 helicopters under the command of Dr Ronald Fleck are heading over the southwestern tip of the island to drop biological weapons on the caves where the rebel forces are stationed."

An outbreak of urgent whispers ran round the cavern. "After that," the reporter continued, "they intend to continue eastward towards Crown Colony, where…" – he paused to look at his watch – "if the ruling council fail to comply with his ultimatum and withdraw their threat of intervention in Colony Island affairs – they intend to drop their oblivion bomb."

The reporter leant forward and confided in his viewers: "We are now able to take you over to the chief minister's house on Colony Island where our roving reporter has managed to secure another interview with Reginald Machin."

Jeremy Stirfry spoke in hushed tones, like an intrepid wildlife reporter about to take a close camera shot of an angry tiger. "The chief minister of Colony Island, Mr Reginald Machin, has agreed to be interviewed in his private apartments. I am on my way now, as you see. Along this corridor. Through these double doors. Through another set of doors. Ah! Good afternoon, Mr Machin! Please don't get up! My photographer can get a good view of you just where you are. Perfect."

"That's Lavinia," whispered Josh. She sat upright just behind her stepdad, looking like the ideal daughter. She must be still in favour! She held her head high and smiled like a statue.

Reginald Machin reclined in an armchair treating the cameramen to his mocking, crocodile smile. "I called you here, Mr Stirfry, to deliver my ultimatum. So, let's get on with it."

"Ah yes, an ultimatum to the ruling council in Crown Colony, I believe."

Machin's face came into full view. "I understand that the council has chosen to ignore my warning," he said in a voice which suggested that he was the only reasonable man present. "I have only one piece of advice for Magnus Maxtrader, who presides over that council. The whole world is watching you. Unless I receive a clear indication that you have made the necessary arrangements to restore food to our shops and cancel any plans you may have made to lend support to the unelected rebels on my little island, I will give my helicopters the order to attack and bomb you to oblivion."

Josh studied Lavinia's face. He thought she blinked once at the mention of her granddad. She must be thinking of her mum, but her face was still a mask.

The reporter was speaking again. "I have just been informed that this interview took place five minutes ago. No official response from Crown Colony, so I suppose we can assume that the deadline has expired. Ah! Apparently, there has been an informal reply from Magnus Maxtrader, who chairs the island council. His message is…Let me read it to you." The announcer paused to unfold the paper which had landed on his desk. He raised his eyebrows. "Let's just say he won't budge."

"He could do something to help!" whispered Megs. "What about his granddaughter?"

"Machin will drop his bomb anyway," whispered Josh.

"Yes, I know but – sh!"

"I'm hearing now from one of our own helicopters hovering above the southern tip of Colony Island. No sign of any helicopters as yet. Oh, yes! Here they are. Three of them. Not quite the three hundred we had been warned about but still a threat in terms of their payload."

Laughter erupted round the cavern, but Sandy whispered, "It was never going to be three hundred. My dad says they haven't got that many. Three is all they need."

"Sh!"

The laughter died down now. A few pirates stared at the roof of the cavern expecting the bombs to burst through, a few hunched their shoulders and shut their eyes, but many more puffed up their chests and looked around them as if to say, "We're part of the rebel army; nothing scares us."

The reporter's voice quivered with excitement. "Have you got a good view of them, Jonny? Ah yes! We're getting a very clear picture of them now. Three helicopters emerging from the cloud. Yes, I can see them all. One. Two. Three. They are diving towards the southwestern tip of the island. And that's the rebel encampment. I can't see any sign of their army yet. But the helicopters will soon be directly overhead."

Some of the rebel soldiers in the cavern exchanged knowing glances.

"They are hovering above the camp. And what's happening now? Are those bombs they're dropping? Small silver bombs. Hundreds of them. Let's see if we can get a closer look at the encampment. No sign of life, at the moment. They must be hiding. Not that this will give them much protection against biological weapons…"

Josh shuddered.

"We've got a very good view of the helicopters now. Yes, three of them. The captain of the lead helicopter seems to be waving at us. Let me just see if I can bring that picture up closer. Yes, do you see that? That's Ronald Fleck. He's giving us the thumbs up sign. He's off again, and the others are following him, in an easterly direction; towards Crown Colony, I suppose."

Josh strained to see the grey dots in the sky carrying their awful load towards Crown Colony; only a few more minutes. He couldn't see anything; just the blue sky. Then at the bottom of the screen the three helicopters swung into focus again.

A note of surprise entered the reporter's voice. "Just watch that lead helicopter! What's he doing now? I don't understand this at all. He's making a rapid ascent. And he's turning. Yes, he's turning back towards his colleagues. What's he doing? A change of direction perhaps? No! He's firing at them. He's actually firing at his two colleagues! And they're down. Both of them. Look! Both machines are on fire, twisting and turning into the ocean. And where's Fleck? He's ascending again. Up, up, up. He's gone into the clouds. I'm afraid we've lost him…I think it's all over. Well, it is now! He's deliberately turned on his own forces and made his escape."

"I think it's all over!" repeated Megs at the top of her voice. "Well, it is now!"

She threw herself on Josh in the crowded cavern, punching and hitting him on his shoulder and gasping out the words, "I think it's all over! Well, it is now!"

Behind them, the whole cavern erupted in laughter and cheers. The party in charge of security unblocked the entrance to the cave and Sandy's dad returned, dangling a silver bomb in one hand. He held it up so that everyone could see the logo imprinted on its side; a lopsided smiley face with the single word 'Fleck' printed in the centre. "They are just balloons," he said. "Party balloons! I think you can take it that it's safe to go outside."

Josh did his best to smile and celebrate with the rest but the desperate mission he had in mind stopped the smile from reaching his eyes.

CHAPTER NINETEEN

L avinia sat having lunch with her stepdad when the helicopters flew off on their fatal mission. She sprang from her chair and made a hysterical attempt to look excited. "Don't you want to hear the news, Daddy?" she cried. "In a few minutes, they will be flying over the rebel camp!" *The boy was in the rebel camp and all she could do was hope.*

Reginald Machin snapped his fingers and accepted a glass of water from one of the four uniformed waiters standing behind his chair. He stared straight ahead of him, glassy-eyed and triumphant. "I make the news, Slug. I am not obliged to listen to it." He looked mad and dangerous. From time to time, he fished from his pocket the marbled form of Saintly diminished to the size of a chess piece. He polished it with a felt rag and held it up to the light. From his other pocket, he retrieved two silver keys; the keys to cells 31 and 32. He dangled them in the air for Lavinia to see. "The boy's parents," he said with a conspiratorial wink. "I can't let them escape again! We'll haul them up in a moment for the execution. The drinks are prepared and then our dear friend, Saintly, will have some company." He brought the keys in one hand together with the marbled form of Saintly in the other, to do a little dance on the table top.

"Still, I might be tempted to hear the news in a few minutes," he conceded, putting the three objects back in his pockets. "I'd like to see when they drop the first oblivion bomb on Crown Colony. That should be fun." He looked up and glared at Maria, who had entered the family dining room unannounced.

"Maria!" He rose from his seat. "How dare you enter this room without knocking?"

"Yes, sir. I'm very sorry, sir. This parcel's just arrived by registered mail. You are supposed to sign for it, sir."

"I have no intention of signing anything. It might be a bomb. Just take it outside and open it."

Lavinia shyly raised a hand. "If she opens it, it might explode in her face."

Her stepdad didn't seem to be listening. He'd gone back to playing with his chess piece and his two keys. "Whose face?" he asked.

"Hers."

He toyed with his dancing keys. "Well, it's worth a try."

"But if it kills her, you'll have nobody to type your letters and all that stuff."

He looked up. "Oh yes, Maria. Maybe we should approach this parcel with care. Does it tick?"

Maria grinned. "No, sir. I don't mind opening it. I think it's just a box, sir."

Her stepdad nodded and put his objects away. "Very well, then. He crouched behind his chair and put a finger in each ear. He waited until the box was opened before unblocking his ears. "What is it?" he shouted, standing up and peering across the table.

Maria wore a puzzled frown. "I don't know, sir. It's a present from Dr Fleck. It looks like red snooker balls to me."

Her stepdad came round and had a look. "My God! Six oblivion bombs! What's he doing sending bombs through the post?"

"He's sent you a letter, sir."

He stared at her as if she were mad. "Well, read it! What does he say?"

Maria stood in the doorway and started reading the letter in a slow, sing-song voice. "He says 'Dear Mr Machin, as promised, I am sending you six completed versions of the oblivion bomb. I would suggest storing them in a cool, dry place. Your snooker table would be ideal, especially as I removed six red balls at my last visit.

I expect you want to know how I am. I am sure you will be glad to hear that I am well and prospering. Assuming control of the bomb project has been an exciting career move for me. But I kept thinking to myself, what's really in it for me? And then I found the answer. You'd have to be mad to imagine that the juice of a flower could be converted into the contents of a bomb but I can assure you that the distilled liquid is making great inroads into the medical trade. It seems that people just can't get enough of it.

I did promise to assemble your gun parts. Unfortunately, I received a better offer. Magnus Maxtrader has accepted delivery of the whole consignment at a very reasonable price. I am not sure if he is aware that the merchandise comes from his own factories on Discovery Island. Still, that's business for you.

I am sorry that I couldn't stop by and say goodbye but I can't help thinking of poor Mr Mole and his place on your mantelpiece.

Incidentally, I hear on the grapevine that it was not Mr Mole who revealed your secrets to the world but your own colleague, Saintly-Smith. It was his idea to warn the pirate bankers and he received a tidy sum of money for his pains. What's more, he planted bugs all over your private apartments. Anyway, I hope you enjoy your bombs as much as I enjoyed inventing them. Think of me on my next cruise, as I'm sure you will, enjoying the fruits of my ill-gotten gains.

Yours Ever,

Ronald Fleck'."

Maria stuffed the folded letter in Lavinia's hand and ran. Lavinia edged towards the open door herself, marvelling at the transformation on her stepdad's face. His cheeks had gone puce, his eyes darted in all directions, froth trickled from his lips. He stared around him with unseeing eyes. "Is that it? Find me a gun, someone. Any gun will do. A pistol. I think I've got a loaded pistol in my bedroom. Under the pillow." Nobody moved. The four uniformed waiters behind the table tried to blend in with the wallpaper. He started to pace the room like a cornered tiger, locked up in his own rage. "I'm going to shoot that man. No, shooting's too good for him. I'll think of something. I'll…" – he turned on Lavinia – "Where are those bugs? For goodness sake, I asked you to find me a pistol. It's not that difficult, surely? At least I can get my revenge on the bugs. And then, Fleck. I'll wipe that face off his Fleck." He shook his fist. "I'll tell you something, Fleck, when I'm finished with you! …That's it! I know what I'll do. I'll track him down and bomb him to oblivion. With snooker balls. Aghh! Help me someone. I can't breathe."

Behind the table, a visitor had just arrived. Lavinia noticed the long, lean figure of Draco. His dark eyes searched the room until he saw her in the doorway. He had a tape in one hand and a cardboard box under his arm. Lavinia began to shake. "I'll get that pistol," she stammered and rushed out of the room.

CHAPTER TWENTY

J osh knew his parents were in danger when he saw that mad dictator with the two silver keys dancing on the table top. His fingers closed round the stone.

The stone seized him. It pulled him into a dark void, sending him hurtling into the unknown, on a roller-coaster ride through time and space. He knew he was heading for the end of the line. But then, as suddenly as it started, the movement slowed.

"It's a journey of four hundred years," said a quiet voice. At the sound of that voice, his fears left him. He sat at his own kitchen table and the voice came from a slim lady with silky black hair, who stood with her back to him, staring at the broken glass in his kitchen window. For a moment he mistook her for his mother, but her shoulders were wider, and she seemed an inch or two taller.

"You've come a long way," said the lady. "I'm your ancestor, Matilda, as you probably guessed. You were right about that mist; it wasn't helping us anymore, was it? And now you must try and rescue your parents. Think hard about this. I wouldn't wish this much danger on anyone. Are you prepared to take the risk?"

He nodded.

She dropped something soft in his hand. "I've brought you this magic wool," she said. "You'll need it when you confront that madman. It's called 'spin'." She laughed. "The stone you've got there is the stone of truth, but truth means nothing to a man like that. In the modern age you need to polish the truth with spin. Let's call it the power to create illusions. After all, what was my mist, if not an illusion?"

Josh sat there after she'd gone, staring at a few threads of golden wool in the palm of one hand. In the other hand, he held his onyx stone. The last of its three flecks had vanished.

Sandy and Megs came into the airport café and sat beside him.

"My parents," he whispered. "I've got to rescue them."

Megs stared out of the window. He knew what she was thinking. A few soldiers walked past. Beyond them, on the runway, three helicopters stood idle. Beyond that lay open fields stretching southward to the outskirts of the Last Resort.

"Where did you see them?" she asked.

"I didn't," Josh said, absorbed in his vision, "but I saw HIM. And I know what he plans to do with them. He's got the keys to their cells."

Megs tugged at his sleeve. "Why didn't you tell me before?"

He struggled to describe what he'd seen. "It happened a moment ago when I shut my eyes. I saw a flash of light and then this madman planning their execution. He's holding them captive in his house."

"Obviously, we have to save them!"

Josh looked across at Sandy. "What would your dad say?"

Sandy thought about it. "He'd say no way." He thought some more and added, "He'd probably take longer to say it. He'd say that the town is still occupied by the enemy, that General Hawkspoon's army is busy enough just defending the airport, that…"

"All right, Sandy, all right. My parents would say the same if they knew what I intended to do." Josh got up. "But I can't ask them, can I?"

Megs grabbed his arm. "I'm coming too."

Josh knew he couldn't take her all the way; but he'd be glad of her company part of the way. He looked at Sandy. Sandy could bring her back and explain where he'd gone. He had to do the last part on his own. He didn't have a plan; just some strands of magic wool and a belief that luck or the power of the stone would see him through.

Sandy slowly got up.

Josh's hopes soared. "You're coming with us?"

Sandy's freckled face went a shade of pink. "I thought I'd better come," he said, "if you need me. I've got my compass."

"What about your dad? Won't he be mad with you?"

"He'll probably say it was a stupid thing to do. Then he'll say it again and keep on saying it for about a year. My dad doesn't get mad. He gets reasonable, if you know what I mean."

Josh nodded. "Let's go."

Luckily, most of the troops were stationed on the other side of the airport, guarding the entrance roads. That's why the three of them were able to skirt the perimeter of the runway without being seen and slip under a barbed wire fence into a soggy wheat field merging into a mile of similar fields, divided by hedgerows and sloping towards the outskirts of town.

"There's still time," Josh called over his shoulder. He had to believe it. He cut a swathe through the wheat, obsessed by a single vision. "It's only about a mile!" he cried. "A few more fields and we've made it."

He broke into a run and the others followed. He struggled through a gap in a hedge at the end of the field, crossed a path and into the next field and ran on and on, stopping now and then to get his breath back and let the others catch up. Finally, he came to a stile leading into a field of yellow rape. He stopped and pointed. "You see that white building? It's a garage. I remember it. It stands at the end of a long lane leading all the way down to the central avenue."

"Have you seen them yet?" asked Megs, holding her right side and panting. "I mean with that stone thing?"

"I haven't tried," Josh admitted. The thought unsettled him. "I'm sure they're alive," he added, determined to believe it. "We just have to get there as fast as we can." He broke into a run again, reassured by the sound of Megs jogging along behind. Sandy was some way back, but he waved and lumbered after them.

They stopped where the fields ended in the grassy verge of the garage forecourt. An army lorry stood parked beside the petrol pump and a bicycle lay next to it on its side. They stood and stared through the evening drizzle down a long, sloping lane, lined by a scattering of small, white bungalows.

"Careful!" whispered Josh. "Do you see that pub further down on our left? There's a bunch of soldiers hanging outside. I have to get past them somehow."

"Too late," said Megs. "They're waving at us! They must be ours."

Josh looked at the lorry. "I suppose that's how they came here. They were probably sent to pick us up. That was quick!"

"What shall we do?" asked Megs.

Sandy caught up with them. He went over and inspected the lorry. "Definitely one of ours," he said.

"That's great!" cried Megs, waving at the soldiers and making ready to sprint down the down the hill. "They can help us!"

Josh held her back. "It's great and it's not great," he said. "When they know where I'm heading, they are bound to stop me." He made a split-second decision. The difficult bit was explaining it to Megs. He grasped her by the shoulders. "Trust me on this one, Megs," he said. "We've got to split. I want you to stay here with Sandy, explain everything to the soldiers and get reinforcements."

Megs gave him a dark stare. "Where are you going?"

Josh turned and ran towards the bicycle. "I'm going to get myself arrested," he shouted. "It's the quickest way to get an interview with Machin!"

· · · · ● · ● · · · ·

Lavinia ran and ran till she found the only hiding place she knew down that long, red-carpeted corridor. She crouched in the dark, poky broom cupboard waiting for her panting breaths and the beating of her heart to slow. The sudden silence frightened her as much as the first frantic roars of pursuit. It meant they were taking their time. She remembered the drill when one of the servants had gone missing after being caught stealing. Her stepdad had sent men scurrying to guard all the exits and then ordered a slow systematic search, room by room, until the girl was dragged screaming from under her bed. She didn't know what happened to the girl after that, but she remembered her face, half-dead with fear, as they forced her into handcuffs and led her into the room where her stepdad was waiting. That's what they would do to her, but she knew what would happen in her case.

She groped around in the half-darkness to check her hiding place. She patted the cold walls and touched damp plaster covering solid stone. She could stand up and sit down but barely stretch her legs. The cupboard contained a broom and a rolled up carpet propped against the corner, thick with dust and spiders. She stood up and tested the walls one more time, touching the ceiling with the tip of her hands. She had to find a better room, one with more space and clutter, one with more exits.

In the distance, she heard laughter and the creak and thud of shoes heading down the narrow corridor; then the rattle of a door being opened and the deadening of sound as the voices got swallowed up in the room. She reached out a hand to the cupboard latch, ready to make her run, but the distant banging of a door told her they were back in the corridor, heading slowly in her direction. She tried to remember how many more doors they had to open before they came to her room. Not that many; four maybe? Perhaps if one room had doors leading off it, that would delay them long enough for her to sprint round the corner past her bedroom into his private apartments.

"She's not in her bedroom."

"Didn't think she would be!"

Hope drained out of her. These voices came from the other direction, close at hand. Quickly, she had to act quickly! She tugged at the tightly rolled carpet, unfolding it enough to wrap a part of it around herself. She wrestled it to the floor and writhed around to find the best position. Footsteps were approaching the door. She lay still, helpless with fear.

"What's this, a cupboard? Not much space to hide in here."

"Better check it, just in case."

"Nothing there."

"Hold on. Let's not be hasty. Take a look at that carpet. Jackpot, mate! We've just hit the jackpot!"

Lavinia went limp. For a moment it felt like relief, to let all her hopes and fears wash away and be handcuffed and carried away like a corpse. Then she remembered that she was going to die, and all the sweet thoughts of her childhood flooded her mind. She clenched her fists and knew she had to hang on to the tiniest grain of hope, come what may.

· · · · ●· ● ● ·· ·

Megs raced after him and seized the bike by the handlebars. He struggled for a moment, trying to wrestle them from her grasp. The soldiers had broken into a run. They were nearly in calling distance.

"Please, Megs," he pleaded. "It doesn't take both of us. Stay here with Sandy. Tell the soldiers where I've gone. Who knows? If there are enough of them, they may be able to storm the chief minister's house."

Megs face began to crumple.

"Please, Megs."

"I believe in you," she sobbed. "Go quickly before anyone can stop you."

He gave her a quick hug and leapt onto the bicycle, swerving past Sandy with a breathless, "Hi Sandy, Megs will explain," and weaving round the soldiers holding out their arms to stop him. It took all his concentration to keep the bike upright as he lurched and skidded over potholes, hurtling down the steep gradient. Soon their distant shouts were behind him and he was racing down the hill, alone and free – and waiting to be arrested.

Then wham! A solid blow in the midriff took his breath away. He felt himself being lifted in the air by a gigantic arm, while the bike disappeared beneath his legs and swerved and keeled over at the side of the lane.

"I think we've met before," said a snide voice. "What do you think, Osborne?"

Getting his breath back, Josh stood shakily upright, recognising the two men who'd once come to his house to arrest his parents. "You can arrest me," he said.

"I told you he was a mouthy little git, didn't I, Osborne?" said Miggs. "What do you think? Shall we follow his lordship's advice and arrest him or shall we put him out of his misery here and now in this lane?"

"Machin's expecting me," said Josh.

"Well, isn't that nice?" said Miggs. "Arranged a little tea party just for the two of you, has he?"

Josh realised to his surprise that these thugs didn't frighten him anymore. "I don't want to keep him waiting." he said. "I've heard he can get impatient."

"Especially when he wants to kill someone," Miggs finished the sentence for him. "So, what are we waiting for? My car's round the corner." He reached for his phone. "I'll tell him to put the kettle on," he said with a leer.

Josh found himself being blindfolded and roughly bundled into the boot of a car. Huddled and cramped in the dark, he got rattled and bumped down the lane, banging his head on a metal toolbox as the car made a skidding swerve onto the central avenue and bruising his shoulder as it drew to an abrupt halt in the central square.

The boot opened and Osborne lifted him in the air, set him on his feet, dusted him down, and pushed him through the door. "Machin's expecting you," he announced in a rough voice. "My mate will show you the way. You won't be needing a return ticket, know what I mean?"

Josh followed the owner of the snide voice up to the entrance lobby on the first floor, across an echoing empty hall, along a red-carpeted corridor, to the breakfast room where Reginald Machin sat facing the door at the centre of a long table, with a few of his guards seated either side of him, and the less important ones standing behind the table.

"A visitor to see you," said Miggs, pushing Josh into the room.

Reginald Machin laughed like a man who'd lost any marbles he'd ever possessed. He twirled a loaded pistol in his hand. His ruffled hair and the stubble on his chin showed that he'd given up on sleep. But his eyes glittered with mad cunning. The other men in that room were a grey blur.

The mad face wobbled before Josh's eyes. "The boy with the stone," Machin said, twirling his pistol in his direction. "Isn't this nice? Two guests in one day. Have you met my stepdaughter?" He pointed to the fair-haired girl in a black skirt and white blouse trussed up in the chair facing him. "She's not speaking very much at the moment, but she nods when I tell her to." A cloth had been stuffed in her mouth, secured by a bandage tightly tied around her face. "Don't you, Lavinia?" He added. "Let's see you nod for the young gentleman." He tugged a rope attached to her neck and Lavinia nodded furiously, provoking laughter and applause from Machin's henchmen.

Josh came and stood beside her, with one hand in his pocket holding the magic wool. Buoyed up in spite of his fear by the strength of his inner vision, he just stood there and stared. Machin's face stopped wobbling and came into focus.

"I've read about you," said Machin. "You're a legend. Legends are about dead people. That's why I like them. Would you like to be a dead person? If so, I can help you achieve your ambition." He gave his pistol another twirl and lined it up on Josh's face.

Josh looked into his mad eyes. Using all his mental strength, he struggled to get a grip on Machin's distracted mind. In a sudden movement, he tossed the golden threads in his face and watched them vanish in a sparkle of tiny lights.

Machin blinked and his mouth fell open. Josh kept his eyes fixed on his face, keeping him under a tight control like a puppet on a string. He said one word, "Fleck." He pointed to the chair. Machin's eyes followed his gaze. In the seat where Josh was supposed to sit, visible only to themselves, sat the smiling form of Ronald Fleck.

Machin jumped up, waving his pistol in triumph. "At last!" he cried. "Revenge is sweet!" He turned to Josh. "That's Fleck! Where did you find him?"

The form vanished.

Behind Machin's back, shocked voices began to murmur.

Machin only had eyes for Josh. "Bring him back!" he cried, with mad, imploring eyes. "I want him back!"

Josh measured the intensity of his wish. He waited.

"I said bring him back!"

"Then release the girl."

That made Machin mad. "You know nothing about this!" he spluttered. "This is family!" He slid a bullet into his pistol and leaned across the table, waving it in Josh's face. I can kill you, you know."

"Release the girl," Josh repeated, "or Fleck will vanish for ever."

Machin sagged back in his chair. "Release the girl!" he muttered.

Nobody moved.

Machin rose to his full height and turned on his cronies. "I said release the girl!"

Draco ran round the table and began to cut Lavinia loose. Josh was dimly aware of her presence by his side heaving sobs of relief.

Machin sat back in his chair and watched his stepdaughter being set free. "Where's Fleck? You told me you'd bring me Fleck."

Josh hadn't moved from his position. "Clear the room," he said.

Machin's face reddened for another explosion of anger, but he thought better of it and shouted, "Get out of the room, you lot. I have to deal with Fleck."

A sparrow settled on the ledge of the open window. Josh looked at the girl sobbing by his side and stared across the table at the pitiful monster hanging on his words.

"Where's Fleck! You promised you'd give me Fleck!"

Josh pointed at the bird. "Fleck's a shape changer," he explained. "There he is on the window ledge."

Machin's mad eyes needed no convincing. "I knew it!" he cried, leaping over the table and firing a shot at the startled bird, which flew up in the air and settled on the balcony fifty feet away.

"Quickly!" cried Machin. "I think I winged him. Let's follow him out to the balcony."

Josh seized Lavinia by the arm and together they followed Machin down the red-carpeted corridor and through another door that led to the balcony. They found him leaning against the railings. When he turned, his face was wet with tears. "I tried to shoot him!" he moaned, "but he wouldn't stay still. He flew away over there."

"No, he didn't," said Josh. "Haven't you noticed something?"

Machin stared at him open-mouthed.

"Don't you feel a buzzing sound in your head?"

Machin put his hands up to his head and slowly nodded.

"That's Fleck. He's hiding inside your head. You've got him."

A look of mad triumph lit up Machin's face. "I've got him!" he repeated. He held the pistol to his ear and, with a smile of utter satisfaction, squeezed the trigger.

Feeling sick and numb at the trick he'd just played, Josh walked over to the lifeless shape sprawled on the floor and picked up the two keys that had fallen from his pocket. He nodded to Lavinia and pointed to the central square beyond the balcony where he could hear a crowd gathering in answer to the single pistol shot. Together they walked past the prone body of Machin and stared over the railings at the crowd. The words "Machin is dead" started as a whisper and rose to a triumphal shout. "Machin is dead." And then, at the very back of the square, Josh saw a small band of rebel soldiers cutting their way through the crowd. And walking behind the soldiers were Sandy and Megs.

He looked at Lavinia and held up the two silver keys. "I'm going to rescue my parents," he said. "Can you show me to their cells?"

CHAPTER TWENTY-ONE

The house at the edge of the world pulsated with lights and laughter and the chatter of a hundred guests, arriving at the house in laughing groups and spilling into the small back garden where waiters in red Maxtrader jackets with yellow linings hurried round, serving drinks from silver trays. After Machin's death, Josh's stepdad had been acting chief minister for a year and this party marked the end of his term of office. Smoke from the barbecue wafted across the garden, drifting westward across the wilderness which was once the edge of the world.

Josh spotted Megs laughing and chatting with his mum behind the barbecue. They smiled at the guests and piled food on their plates while Sandy and his dad cooked the meat. "You know what you told me a year ago?" Megs was saying. She had to shout to make her voice heard above the noise. "You said that I was living in a mist but that in a year's time I would wake up and find that the mist had cleared. I wonder what you meant by that?"

Josh guessed what his mum meant. Megs didn't look at all like that thin, sulky pirate girl with straggly black hair that he had first met at the hillside farm. He saw Megs nearly every day now. She went to the same school as he did, in the class below his, and she often slept over at weekends.

Sandy emerged, red-faced, from behind the barbecue. Josh saw Sandy every day too. They'd been in the same class since primary school. Sandy didn't do greetings like 'hi' or 'hello' or 'cheers'. He just said what he wanted to say. "You know that lake?" he said.

"I nearly fell in it. Don't you remember?"

"Oh yes." Sandy's eyes looked troubled for a moment, as if he'd just missed a joke. "It's full of fish!" he said. "I mean, I thought fish needed sunlight, right? But before there wasn't any sunlight – not with that mist – so I wonder how they got there."

"Maybe somebody put them there."

"Maybe," said Sandy. He didn't sound convinced.

"It's a year since we last went fishing together," said Josh, "except we didn't, because I waited outside the house and you didn't come. But you came the next day and showed me the way through the mist. Don't you remember?"

"I remember the mist."

"I suppose we could go fishing tonight."

"Maybe. Where are you going?"

"I thought I'd go and look for Lavinia. Are you coming?!

"Maybe later."

Josh picked his way round a circle of suited politicians. He hurried past before anyone could point him out as 'the boy with the stone'.

He found Bertie at the far end of the garden by the white gate talking to Sandy's dad, who'd done with the cooking and held a steaming plate of food in one hand as he listened.

"I'm a civil servant nowadays," Bertie was saying. "Actually, I'm working for the Ministry of Food. I'm not sure how much longer my job will last. When the Flagsmiths took over, they found there was hardly any food left in the shops, so they had to introduce rationing. That's what I do. Hand out food coupons."

"Isn't that a bit like putting a chocaholic in charge of a chocolate factory?" asked Sandy's dad.

Bertie grinned. "Yes, well. In the end we had to make a pact with the devil, in the shape of Magnus Maxtrader, so it looks as if rationing is on the way out. Hello, young Josh. Have you seen my red socks? I thought they'd add a flash of colour to the occasion. What do you think?"

Josh grinned. "They'd be good for cycling after dark," he said.

At that moment, a golden Labrador puppy emerged at their feet, twisting its body in doggy convulsions and thrusting its wet nose into Josh's hands. "This is Cuddles," Bertie explained, adding to its ecstasy by caressing its neck. "It's not mine. It belongs to Lavinia. She must be around somewhere." He looked up and gave a nod of his head in the direction of Lavinia and her mum who were hurrying across the lawn towards them.

Josh hadn't seen Lavinia except for a few days after that time on Machin's balcony. She looked different now, in an arty shirt and an old pair of jeans; as if she wanted to become a teenager again after a long period of captivity. His mum said she'd been through counselling sessions but she'd pulled through, thanks to her tough Maxtrader genes.

Lavinia said 'hi' and gave him a subdued smile. Her mum tapped her lightly on the shoulder and left her, murmuring in Josh's ear, "I'm sure you two have got lots to talk about."

Josh didn't know what to say. She was smiling at him, waiting for him to start.

"You—" he began.

She opened her mouth at the same time. "You—" she said. She stopped and laughed. "You go first," she said.

"I wanted to say you tried to rescue my parents, just like you said you would."

"Yea, tried. And you saved my life. Whew! We got that bit over. What are you doing now?"

"Nothing special; school, a bit of sport, I dunno."

"Not saving the world?" she asked. Her eyes danced with mischief. "I thought that's what Guardians were supposed to do."

"Listen, I only did all that stuff because I had to, and Megs helped me a lot, and Sandy and Bertie and the general and my parents and you, of course. You did more than anyone!"

Lavinia's blue eyes studied his face. "Come on, Josh! I'm not joking now. You did save the world in a way. At least you saved our part of the world."

"What are you doing now?" he asked quickly.

"I go to drama school. It's great. I want to be an actress."

"What, for real?"

She raised her eyes in horror. "No, what I did with my stepdad, that was for real. I'd never want to go through that again. This is make-believe. It's much more fun – and if you're good, you can even get paid for it."

Josh saw Megs heading in their direction, with Sandy a few steps behind. Lavinia spotted her straightaway. "Hi, you must be Megs, and this is Sandy, right? I feel as if I know you, though we've never met, but we've been through so much together – though not together – well, you know what I mean!"

Megs beamed. Sandy looked puzzled.

"I met your granddad once," said Megs. "He said we were as bad as each other."

"Did he? Coming from him that's a compliment. You know he still talks about you? I don't know what you said to him, but you certainly made an impression."

The two girls were soon chatting as if they'd known each other for a long time.

"Here comes our chief minister!" observed Bertie as Josh's stepdad strode forward to join them.

"Steady on!" he protested. "You are talking to the new headmaster of the Sloane School. My last day as 'co-chairperson of the caretaker government' – goodness, what a mouthful! –

finished – let me see, now," – he paused to look at his watch – "five minutes ago."

"Are you sorry about that?" asked Bertie.

"Do I look sorry? I'm delighted! I always said that, in the world of politics, popularity is like sand in an egg timer. With all the unpopular things we had to do – and mistakes too, of course – the sand was running out fast. No! Botany is my field – dealing with strange plants like 'oblivia preciosa'."

"What's happened to Miss Brassmould, then?" asked Bertie. "Our Megs tells me that she has been sent to prison."

"That's not exactly right. At least, she's not a prisoner but a prison warder. We couldn't convict her of any specific crime but we have to keep an eye on her nonetheless. She's in charge of dangerous criminals. Osborne and Miggs are there – in separate cells, of course. I hear they've even taken up needlework."

"Do they like it?" asked Josh.

"Well, let's say it's a choice between that and not getting fed. Draco's there too, of course. He's opted to print off jokes that go in Christmas crackers."

Josh glanced at Lavinia and tried to change the subject. "What about the Cat Lady?" he asked.

His stepdad put a hand on his shoulder. "Ah, now, that is interesting! Rumour has it that she ran off with Dr Ronald Fleck, of all people."

"Haven't you caught him yet?" Bertie asked.

"No, Dr Fleck is bad news. The sort of bad news that won't go away. I'm sure we'll be hearing from him soon."

"Uggh!" Lavinia shuddered. The news seemed to have silenced her.

"I know exactly what you mean," said Josh's stepdad. "You're Lavinia, aren't you? I was hoping I'd get a chance to meet you. Yes – what was I saying? People like Fleck are a stain that won't wash away. You know what I'm most afraid of?" Josh's stepdad cast his earnest eyes around like a schoolteacher anxious to hold the attention of his class. "A pirate backlash; that's what I'm afraid of. I can tell you that it's already started. Once something as evil as Machin or Fleck gets hold of society, it can only lead to more evil. And so the process goes on. It may take years to wash the stain away."

Josh listened with half an ear. With people like Machin and Fleck around, it was no fun being Guardian. But he'd managed with the help of his friends, and he reckoned he could handle the challenges that lay ahead. For the moment, the party was in full swing. After that, his mum had agreed that, when the adults left, he and his friends could stay on and chat in the garden till after midnight and crash out in the big marquee.

THE END

THE GUARDIANS NECKLACE - BOOK 2 IN THE ISLAND WARS

CHAPTER ONE

J osh woke to the smell of canvas and wood smoke and a faint sense of unease. He rubbed his eyes and tried to focus. Where was he? Northwoods Island, camped between the pine woods and the beach.

He reached over and undid the tent flap , catching a sudden blast of cold morning air. The sweet smell of pine wood drifted on the breeze. This was what they had come for! His stepdad had led them on a detour through the woods and found this deserted spot on the northern tip of the island. He and Megs had planned to get up early and explore those woods. He groped around for his watch. Six o'clock. He struggled out of his sleeping bag, pulled back the tent flap and peered through the hanging mist.

Getting up early was Megs' idea. Sometimes, you wouldn't think it, but she was only twelve years old, nearly two years younger than himself. Getting up early was an adventure at that age. He expected to see her peering out of her tent, ready to dash across and wake him.

He stepped outside and stood barefoot on the damp grass and looked around him. He blinked and stared. But he saw no tent and no Megs.

In the place where her tent should have been, he saw a flattened patch of grass and odd strips of canvas attached to bent skewers; beyond that, a white bundle of canvas tossed in a crumpled heap at the edge of the woods.

He threw a coat over his pyjamas and looked around him, shivering in the breeze. There could have been a gale in the night. He thought he'd heard something; more like the sound of animals scampering across the campsite. Or was that part of his dream? He scanned the edge of the woods, hoping to see Megs sitting on her rucksack waiting for him to help her with the tent.

His eyes returned to that white bundle of canvas tossing in the breeze. Somehow it didn't look right. There wasn't enough of it. He raced across the grass to investigate. He pulled the tent away from the trees and ran his hands along the sides of the canvas. It looked as if someone had sliced it away from the groundsheet. Pirates had done this! A year ago, he'd have said colonists. But he hadn't seen any colonists on this strange island. It must have been his own people who'd done this. No sign of the groundsheet! No sleeping bag either! They must have seized the sheet by its four corners and carried Megs off with them, sleeping bag and all, into the woods.

But why Megs? He was the one with the stone. That's what they wanted, of course; not that it would be of any use to them! He raced back to his tent and threw on his clothes, thoughts pounding through his head. Why hadn't they seized him instead? He struggled into his trousers. Socks. Where were his socks? Perhaps they'd tried? Forget about socks. Shoes! Where were his shoes? But he always kept his stone hidden. Of course! That's why they'd gone for Megs. They wanted him to give up his stone to get her free. So they'd contact him soon and tell him where to meet. He stared into the dark woods. They couldn't be far away. Quickly! Finding them first would give him a slight edge. He grabbed his stone; he'd hide it along the way.

His parents had pitched their tent at the edge of the cliff. He ran in, unzipped the sleeping compartment and shouted, "Dad. Wake up!"

His stepdad's startled face rose a few inches from the pillow of his sleeping-bag. He rubbed his eyes and looked around him, passing a hand through his mop of straw hair. "Ham and handlebars," he said, in a faraway voice. "Oh, it's you Josh. You're up early. Off on an expedition somewhere? Good idea." His voice tailed away as his head touched the pillow again.

"Wake up, Dad. This is serious. They've taken Megs. No time to explain!"

This time his stepdad shot up as if he'd been jabbed in the ribs. "Hey, Josh! Wait!"

Josh hardly heard him as he raced away. His stepdad could call the emergency services or whatever. He couldn't wait for that. Megs needed his help now!

Beyond Meg's tent lay a sandy path leading deep into the woods. He sprinted through the pine trees, placed at regular intervals on either side of the path, seeing the way ahead for a hundred yards or so in the flickering light. Then the undergrowth grew denser, blocking his view. He had to slow up. The enemy could be waiting behind any bush or tree.

He stopped at a fork in the path. His instinct told him to take the narrower path on the right which wound out of sight through the undergrowth. He thought of using his stone to know for sure. But there wasn't time. Besides, he knew they'd have taken the wider path on his left; if he took this other path, he had a chance of creeping up on them unseen. He hurried down it, heart beating fast like a hunter afraid of its prey. She couldn't be far away. He stopped for a moment, thinking he heard a human noise; a cough or a muttered word. Then he saw a lighter patch ahead, a space in the trees. This looked like a likely place. He dived into a clump of bushes and edged his way forwards.

Thoughts thumped through his mind again. He had to play for time until help arrived. He had to hide his stone – but keep it in reach. Use it to bargain with but never give it up – something told him those people would kill them both if they got what they came for. The brambles pricked his arms and he could hardly see. Noiselessly, he brushed some branches aside to get a better view.

A large, oblong object stood in the open space. He slowly pushed his way upwards into a standing position and peered down at it through the leaves. He gulped when he realised what they'd done.

Her face stared upwards like a hooked fish from the open end of a shallow, wooden chest. A long steel blade like a paper cutter hung poised across her neck. He clenched the stone in his pocket. What kind of people would do that to a kid like Megs? He braced himself to make a dash from his hiding place and run to her side, but he heard light footsteps approaching down the path. He dropped silently to the ground again and flattened himself among the leaves, struggling to control his breathing.

He saw the figure of a woman out for a walk. He began to breathe normally again. Maybe she could help him? Between them, they could get Megs free – or he could do it himself while the woman went back for help. She'd be here in a minute. He'd ask her. He saw her clearly now; a tall, athletic figure in black jeans and a frilly, white shirt. She had short, fair hair and black, pearl earrings…She…

Just then the woman turned and stared directly at the place where he was hiding. He caught a sudden glimpse of those catlike eyes. She couldn't see him, could she? He gripped the stone in his pocket and stood motionless behind the thin screen of leaves. Those eyes seemed fixed on him; empty, inquisitive, intent on mischief. A casual visitor out for a walk? No chance! This was Catharine Cattermole! The Cat Lady!

Her eyes switched away from him and she was a woman again. She looked out of place in these woods; like a nurse in uniform doing her rounds. He watched, mesmerised, as she settled on the coffin lid.

"Are you comfy in this little bed I've made for you, darling?" she asked in a sweet soft voice, peering down at Megs.

He rose noiselessly to his feet to get a better view. He saw her reach down a hand to finger Megs' neck. She extracted a tissue from her pocket.

"Poor child," she murmured. "You've cut yourself. Let me wipe away the blood for you."

He heard a defiant croak. "Don't touch me!"

The lady's smile flashed a warning. "Let me have a good look at you." He saw Megs flinch, as those teasing eyes inspected her face.

"Poor Megs! How can I make you more comfortable until your boyfriend arrives?"

"I haven't got a boyfriend. Let me go!"

Josh's muscles tightened again as he watched Megs' frightened face, staring upwards like a patient in a dentist's chair, tensing herself against any sudden movement.

"It won't be long now. He'll soon be here. Would you like me to take this metal thing away from your neck?"

"Just do it!"

"Of course, dear!"

Suddenly, she leaned over and touched something on the side of the coffin. He tensed his fists.

"Ow, my throat!"

He choked back the urge to cry out.

Her face was close to Megs' now. Josh caught the quick smile and the tinkling laugh. "Silly me! I touched the wrong button. But it's so tempting, isn't it?" She dabbed Megs' brow and touched another button which made the blade fly upwards an inch. "Don't worry. I'm not going to harm you. You can move your head now. You're free! Well, almost. You see, it's the boy they want. He's got my master's stone and my master needs it."

He heard the relief in Meg's voice as she found she could turn her neck. "The stone belongs to Josh!" she cried. It's the Guardian's stone!"

The Cat Lady stared at her. "You'd think so, wouldn't you? My master thinks it's his!"

"The stone of truth?" Megs snorted. He could see she was past caring now. "What would any friend of yours want with the truth?"

Josh's heart swelled with pride for Megs and her bravery. He held his breath, fearing that some terrible punishment would follow. Instead, he noticed a glint of satisfaction in the Cat

Lady's eyes. She turned away as if she had other things on her mind. Then she was back again with a plan. "I see you're getting cross. I think it's time to call the boy. Maybe he can help us both."

Josh's hands rushed to his pockets. He had to silence that phone. Then he remembered with relief that he had forgotten to bring it with him. Would his dad go to the tent and pick it up? What would he say? And what kind of help would he summon up and when?

She sat upright and tapped out the numbers on her phone. She held it in her hand a long time. She turned to Megs. "Strange. He must be a heavy sleeper, your boyfriend. Oh, hello. That's Mr Flagsmith, isn't it? … That's right. Catharine Cattermole…Yes, the PE teacher at your school. A long time ago. How time flies when you're busy!... No, don't say anything. I'd like to speak to Josh if you don't mind. Well, really! There's no need to be offensive. I am sure we can work this out amicably. I've got a young lady here who's in a bit of a fix. Yes, Megs. She's under my protection. Listen!" The Cat Lady pointed a finger at Megs and poked it in her eye.

Megs shrieked. The sudden jolt caused her to raise her head and cut her neck again on the blade.

"You see? I told you not to say anything. Megs needs your help straightaway. So, tell Josh to come quickly and he may be able to save her. It's very easy. I can see your tents over there near the shore. Just tell him to follow the path behind you into the woods. When he gets to the fork, he's to turn left. He will see us just a little further on, relaxing in a little glade. At least, I'm relaxing. I don't know about Megs. No! Don't try to follow him or you'll put both their lives in danger. We don't want that, do we? Sorry, I can't hear you… I'll take that as a no…. Oh! And – silly me! – I almost forgot. Tell him to bring his stone. That's all we require of him. I'm sure you'll be able to make him see sense."

The Cat Lady disappeared in the direction of the tents. She probably aimed to lie in wait for him at the edge of the glade.

Josh hesitated. He looked through the bushes in the direction where the Cat Lady had gone. He felt a wrench in his stomach as he parted with his stone, hiding it in the mud beneath his feet. He covered it with leaves and raced into the open to kneel beside the coffin.

"Megs," he whispered. "Sh! Stay still! No! Megs, don't move or you'll hurt yourself."

He saw her pale, trapped face tremble with relief.

He followed with his eyes the intricate wiring of the buttons attached to the side of the coffin. A sticker with a lopsided smiley face caught his eye for a second. He pressed the lower button. The steel blade sprang back a little.

"Careful, Josh!"

"Don't worry, Megs. I'll be careful. I'll have you free in seconds."

"She's coming back!"

"Only a second." He pressed the lower button one more time, but nothing happened.

"Just do it!" she screamed. Her limbs had gone rigid with desperation.

This time he pressed harder. The guillotine gave a little judder and then a click. Suddenly he saw the blade rise a full six inches from her neck.

"I'm free! I'm free!" cried Megs, bursting into tears. "I can move my head. I'm free!"

"Stay still, Megs! Freeze! It's not over yet." He reviewed his handiwork. "Look Megs, this is the best I can do. I am going to haul you out. Just keep your head away from that blade." Holding her by the shoulders, he used all his strength to extricate her frozen body from the coffin and drag her like a limp fish onto the ground. She hopped and stumbled around in joy, hugging him until he gasped aloud for breath.

"What about your stepdad?" she whispered.

"He knows!"

"Have you got the stone?"

"She's not getting it. Sh!"

"I knew you'd come! They told me they wanted your stone!"

"Weren't you scared?"

"Of course, I was scared, but I knew it wasn't for ever."

"How are you feeling now?"

Her eyes widened. "Wonderful! I feel wonderful!" she said.

"Sh!"

The sound of a cracking twig prompted him to look up. Maybe he should have kept his stone with him after all. A group of soldiers had materialised from nowhere and formed a circle around the coffin.

"Stay there! Don't move!" A tall pirate with a hooked nose and joyless eyes came and stood over him. He wore a ragged dark green pullover smelling of sweat and pipe tobacco. Josh looked beyond him at the other soldiers, sheathed daggers hanging from their belts, legs apart, chests puffed out, staring.

"So you're the pirate Guardian, the boy with the stone," said the man, staring at Josh with loathing. "Your father's an important man in these parts, I hear. I suppose that's how he fixed your selection. You're not the only pirate to be born with the 'gift' as they like to call it. Where I come from, we don't hold with Guardians. What can you do for us besides prophesy and preach peace?" He pointed to the scar running down the side of his right cheek. "A colonist did this to me. And he wasn't preaching peace, I can tell you."

A few of the soldiers nudged one another and laughed.

With Megs at his side, Josh felt brave. He kept his arm around her shoulders and stared at the opposition. They wore combat fatigues but they didn't look like soldiers. Why no guns? Two of them were old men. They shuffled their feet and turned away from his stare. There was one boy, probably not much older than himself, who hung his head and stared at his boots. If he'd got his stone, maybe he'd have the strength to get inside their heads. But he couldn't risk fetching it from its hiding place.

Just then, a fat balding man lit a cigarette. He had 'The Rebel Prince' printed on his shirt. Who was this 'Prince'? He must be a pirate; only pirates gave themselves names like that.

The men stiffened to attention. The Cat Lady had returned. She walked through them, swinging her hips, as if they didn't exist, with a gleam of command in her eyes. "Ah, Josh!" she said in a teasing voice. "The young Guardian! The boy with the gift! Mind you, your famous 'gift' is not much use in a tight situation like this."

Josh knew from the mischievous glitter in her eyes that she'd found his weak spot. If she could bring on a fit with her taunting, she'd get what she came for. "I thought you worked for the colonists," he said, loud enough for her followers to hear. "Killing pirates used to be your thing."

He knew as soon as he said it that words cut no ice with these pirates. One or two of them stared at the ground, but they'd made their decision, and nothing would budge them now. The Cat Lady herself just smiled. "Go on," she said. "Talk. What else can you do; froth at the mouth and have visions. Well, I suppose your stone would give you strength – but I see you're looking worried so maybe you haven't got it with you!"

She came close enough to smile at him. Then her eyes flickered away again as if she'd lost interest. She turned and waved a dramatic arm at the circle of soldiers. "I would like to introduce you to my friends. Of course, you will be glad to know that they are all pirates like yourself. Well, not quite like yourself, actually. They come from Windfree; the island of peace and freedom where my master rules."

Who was her master? He thought of that smiley face on the coffin. Just the sort of cynical logo that would appeal to Ronald Fleck! But did he live in Windfree? He wasn't a pirate. Nor was the Cat Lady. Maybe that was the connection. He suppressed a shudder.

The Cat Lady was speaking to Megs now. She pointed to her soldiers. "There you are," she said, "'Peace and Freedom' – it's printed on their shirts."

Megs scowled. "Is that the kind of freedom you offered me in that coffin thing?" she asked.

"Freedom requires the occasional sacrifice," said the Cat Lady. You could tell she was getting bored with the conversation. "I am afraid my friends here are becoming impatient." She stared at Megs with her cruel, fathomless eyes. "Just ask your boyfriend to fetch me his stone, dear, and we'll all be happy."

"Some of us will be dead," said Megs, gripping Josh's arm.

"And I haven't got the stone," added Josh, "But I can tell you where to find it."

The Cat Lady's eyes sparkled with interest. "Better search him Walter, just in case. He may be telling the truth. In that case it won't be far away."

The pirate in the green pullover loomed over him. "Shirt," he said, extending a large, calloused hand.

Josh fumbled with his shirt.

"Shoes. You can give me your socks, too."

Josh stood in his bare feet.

Walter held out his hand again. "Trousers!" he commanded.

"Come off it!" cried Megs. "You can see he hasn't got it!"

Walter stared at Josh and reached for his long knife which he pointed at his midriff. "Do you want me to cut them off?" he asked.

Josh handed over his trousers and watched as Walter ripped open the pockets, letting his watch and a few coins spill onto the grass. He stood in his underpants, feeling as useless as a skinned frog.

"What about the girl?" asked Walter.

The Cat Lady shook her head. "No, the boy's the one, but he hasn't got it. We must help him remember where he put it." Josh could feel Megs tighten her hold on his arm. They both knew they were safe until the Cat Lady got what she came for. The pirates began to mutter among themselves and one or two reached for their knives.

The Cat Lady whispered something to Walter. She approached Josh again, all charm and sweetness. "I know how you feel, Josh. You want to put up a bit of a show in front of your girlfriend here. But what's the point? We'll get what we came for in the end."

Josh heard the distant sound of a helicopter landing in the woods. His heart beat faster at the prospect of rescue. The Cat Lady observed his reaction and smiled. "Reinforcements, no doubt; ours, not yours," she said. "So I am going to ask you again, nicely, one more time. Give me the stone."

Josh stared at her. Could she be bluffing? He had to keep a firm grip on the voice of reason. His stepdad would have called for help. It had to be on its way.

She had already lost interest in him. She had another plan on her mind. As she stood back and studied them, a smile formed at the corners of her mouth. "Now, are you ready, Megs? Yes, I'm sure Megs can help us."

"Don't touch her!" exclaimed Josh, standing between them.

Megs clung to his arm. "Don't bother to try and stop her! That's what she's after. She's a cat. That's her game."

The Cat Lady turned to her soldiers. "Walter Smearing," she called out. The man in the green pullover gave a knowing grin. "I hear you are handy with a knife. If Megs would favour us by standing against this tree."

Josh made a sudden lunge as he saw two pirates manhandling her and dragging her away. Two other pirates quickly grabbed him from behind and a sweaty arm lay across his windpipe, almost throttling him.

"You'll never get your wretched stone!" Megs cried as they shoved her against a pine tree and started lashing a rope around her arms and legs. "Don't try to stop them!" she shouted at Josh. "They're just looking for an excuse to beat you up."

Josh writhed, hot and breathless, in the hands of his captors. He watched as each pirate unsheathed his knife and laid it at Walter's feet. Then they stood back and waited for a word from the Cat Lady who stood in the centre of the glade.

"There's only one problem," said Josh, thinking fast on his feet. "I gave Megs the stone and only she knows where it's hidden."

The Cat Lady looked at him with amusement. "I don't believe you, Josh, but I'm willing to test your theory. Now remember, Walter, you are not supposed to kill her because she may have some information for us. So, let's start with the arms. And maybe, after the first throw, she will suddenly remember where she put the stone or Josh will remember for her."

Josh saw Megs struggling with the ropes that cut into her arms. Walter stood barely six feet away. He couldn't miss!

"You're not much of a knife-thrower!" he taunted him. "Stand further back. Even I couldn't miss from that distance."

Walter didn't seem to hear him. Just then, Josh wriggled from the pirates' grasp and made a sudden lunge, trying to kick the knife from the pirate's hand. It was useless. The two pirates grabbed him again and dragged him to the edge of the circle. An elbow in his neck made him gasp for breath. Megs began to shake and sob. He went dizzy, watching her. Perhaps if he gave them the stone? Even in his desperation, he knew that wouldn't work. Once he told them where he'd hidden it, they were both as good as dead. "Don't worry, Megs!" he shouted. "Help's on its way. You'll see!"

The Cat Lady ignored him. "Are you ready, Walter?" she asked.

Walter wiped the blade on his jeans.

"You can throw when I give the word."

Walter nodded.

He saw it all in slow motion, like a scene pictured underwater. Everybody had gone still. Walter had raised his arm in readiness. The Cat Lady watched intently, all eyes upon her.

"Now!"

Josh jerked backwards. It was a while before he dared look up. Megs stood rigid, as if expecting the knife, but her chest heaved in quick pants and he couldn't see any blood. The pirates had gone very quiet. All eyes had switched to the knife-thrower. Walter Smearing's body had fallen forward like a useless sack, blood seeping from a hole in his head. The soldiers stood and stared at him, shocked and motionless. Even the Cat Lady looked confused.

Pistol fire rang out from the bushes on Josh's right.

"Get down! All of you! Get down!"

Nobody moved.

The bushes parted and two soldiers burst out of the wood; a giant of a man with a bald head and a moustache and a much shorter man who spoke with the calm certainty of being obeyed. "Down on the ground! Hands in front of you! Don't move!" he said in a matter-of-fact voice. He fired one shot in the air and said "That's better. Keep your heads down."

"That could have been you," he said to the Cat Lady. "No, don't smile. On the ground. Yes, you, too! Hands in front of you!"

He turned to Josh and said "Get down! Don't worry about Megs. Leave her! I'll attend to that."

He walked over and cut Megs free. Neither he nor his friend took much notice of the pirates, who lay prone on the ground. He strode over to Josh and pulled him to his feet. "Hi, Josh," he said, giving him a firm handshake, "I'm Captain Ketch. I'm in charge of this little operation. And that's Sergeant Jenkins. You're free to walk around now. These people aren't going anywhere. God knows why they didn't think to carry any firearms but I'm not complaining. You can make yourself useful by collecting up all their knives. You might want to recover your clothes too, before he bleeds all over them. Jenkins here will shoot anyone who dares to move. That one over there, maybe? He's reaching for his knife. Freeze! Withdraw your hand! That's right!"

Soon there was just one large sergeant with a pistol, sitting on a log and taking playful aim at the Cat Lady and the nine remaining pirates spread-eagled on the ground. He cracked a few jokes, but no one doubted that the bullets in his pistol were real.

"What will you do with the prisoners?" Megs asked the captain.

The captain faced her, hands on hips. "You're Megs, aren't you? A brave girl, I saw that."

Josh thought he saw most things.

"The Cat Lady's coming with us. In fact, you can handcuff her yourself, Megs. You'd like that, wouldn't you?"

Megs grinned.

"Miss Cattermole," the captain called out. "Stand over there by that tree! Never mind the smile. It's wasted on me, I'm afraid." He handed Megs the handcuffs. "Hands behind your back. There. Megs, you can do the rest. Tie her legs too. Loosely, mind. We're taking her with us."

"What about the rest of them?" asked Josh, struggling with the rope.

"The rest? Have you got all those knives? Good. Give them to me. I'll take care of them. After that, we'll just leave them. I doubt they're capable of doing us much harm. Very soon, the whole forest will be crawling with their army – if you can call it that – so we have no time to lose. We'll make a dash for the helicopter and get out of here before reinforcements arrive. How does that plan suit you, Megs?"

Josh knew what her answer would be.

"It sounds brilliant," she whispered, beaming.

Donald, his wife Joey, and George, the very demanding collie.

Donald Frank Brown was born in Inverness, Scotland, in 1943 during the second world war. In his gap year, before studying English at Exeter College, Oxford, he worked in Paris selling the New York Times outside the Louvres. After teaching English in Brighton and the United Nations school in New York, he settled in Jersey and founded a language school. He is married with three children, ten grandchildren and one great grandchild.

The Guardian's Necklace - The Island Wars Book 2

The Neustrian Princess - The Island Wars Book 3

Printed in Great Britain
by Amazon